The Hardy Boys®
in
Cave-In

Other Hardy Boys® Mystery Stories in Armada

The Hardy Boys® Mystery Stories

Cave-In

Franklin W. Dixon

Illustrated by Paul Frame

Armada

First published in the U.S.A. in 1983 by
Wanderer Books, a division of Simon & Schuster, Inc.
First published in the U.K. in 1983 by
Angus & Robertson (U.K.) Ltd, London.
First published in Armada in 1984 by
Fontana Paperbacks, 8 Grafton Street, London W1X 3LA.

Printed and bound in Great Britain by
Anchor Brendon Ltd, Tiptree, Essex

Contents

1 Kidnapped!

Eighteen-year-old Frank Hardy flipped the dial on the television set, then sat down at the kitchen table to finish his supper and watch the evening news.

"We don't have time for that," said his brother Joe, who was a year younger. "We're supposed to pick up the girls in half an hour. The show starts at eight."

It was the first night of the Hardys' winter vacation from Bayport High, and they were planning to celebrate by taking their dates, Callie Shaw and Iola Morton, to the movies.

"Shh!" Frank said quickly, his attention focused on the news program. "I want to hear this."

On the television screen appeared the picture of a well-known movie star, Richard Chase. Frank and Joe had seen the handsome actor in several recent films.

"Richard Chase is believed to have been abducted from his Los Angeles home sometime this afternoon," the reporter announced. "Currently, he has been working on a new film, *Horror Hotel*, a thriller about a monster that terrorizes the winter vacationers in a remote mountain lodge.

"Evidently," the anchorman continued, "Mr. Chase is now involved in horrors of a very real kind. The police are investigating the actor's mysterious kidnapping, but have yet to come up with any leads in the case."

Just then, Frank and Joe heard a loud gasp from behind them. They turned to look at their Aunt Gertrude, who was standing near the door with her mouth open and her eyes as wide as saucers.

"What's the matter, Aunty?" Frank asked.

"He called here this morning!" Miss Hardy, who had lived with the family for some time, replied, nearly coughing out the words.

"Who called?" Joe spoke up.

"Mr. Chase! I didn't know he was the movie

star, though. I thought he was just another one of your father's clients. So I took down the message and—"

"He didn't speak to Dad?" Joe interrupted.

"No, your father was out, so I wrote down the caller's name and number and told him that I would pass it on to Fenton when he came home."

Fenton Hardy was a famous private detective, who had once been on the New York Police Department. Frank and Joe were following in his footsteps as amateur detectives and had already built up an excellent reputation for themselves.

"Are you sure it was *the* Richard Chase who called?" dark-haired Frank asked. He was thinking that there were probably hundreds of people in the country with the same name.

"He didn't say, but it's too much of a coincidence," Aunt Gertrude declared. Just then, they heard the front door open and close. "I think your father is here now," she added.

A few seconds later, Fenton Hardy entered the kitchen. "Can you two have your things packed in ten minutes?" he asked his sons in a serious tone. "And take some clothing for extremely cold weather. We'll have to make an eight-thirty flight to Los Angeles. I'll explain later." With that, he left the kitchen and rushed upstairs to pack his own bags.

"I guess it *was* Richard Chase the movie star," Frank said as he downed the last of his milk and stood up from the table. Then both brothers ran up the stairs after their father.

"What about our dates with Iola and Callie?" Joe asked, throwing up his hands.

"I'll call them right now," Frank replied. "They'll understand."

A few minutes later, the boys put their clothes into suitcases, and in no time were packed and ready to go. Their mother, who had been taking a nap in her bedroom, was already outside starting the car. "I'm driving you to the airport," she said.

The boys were about to climb into the car, when Aunt Gertrude appeared, shaking a finger at them. "I want you two to be careful," she said. "You have a knack for attracting trouble like flowers attract honeybees."

"Don't worry, Aunty," Joe said, and gave her a big kiss.

But Aunt Gertrude knew there would be trouble, as there always was when her nephews tackled a mystery. She was very fond of them and was afraid that someday their sleuthing would endanger their lives. Actually, it often had.

On their way to the airport, Fenton Hardy told his sons that Richard Chase had phoned him the night before. The star was apparently on to something illegal involving the movie he was working in, but he wanted Mr. Hardy to come to Los Angeles before disclosing any of the details.

"I was planning to go to the West Coast in a couple of days," the detective went on. "But on my way home tonight, I heard the news report that Chase had been kidnapped. So I want to get there as soon as possible."

"We saw the story on television," Frank said. "Then Aunt Gertrude told us that Mr. Chase had called again this morning when you were out."

"It seems he really knew something," Mr. Hardy said. "So his enemies abducted him before he could tell anyone."

"Why did you want us to come along?" Frank inquired.

"I suspect that Chase's captors, whoever they are, know that he contacted me. So I might have a hard time from now on learning what's happening."

"I get it," Joe said. "We can act as undercover agents, so to speak."

Mr. Hardy nodded. "As I said, Chase told me his information had something to do with the movie *Horror Hotel*. If you two could somehow land jobs on the set, we would stand a better chance of getting to the bottom of this case."

Mrs. Hardy's sparkling blue eyes registered concern as she pulled into the airport terminal. Like Aunt Gertrude, she was worried. "Please don't let the boys get involved in anything too dangerous," she pleaded, looking at her husband.

"Don't worry, Mom," Joe answered for his father. "We can take care of ourselves."

All three hugged Mrs. Hardy, then hurried inside to make the eight-thirty plane to California.

The flight took six hours, but because of the three-hour time difference it was still before midnight when they landed at the Los Angeles airport.

The first thing the boys noticed when they got off the plane was the weather. Although it was late December, and freezing cold back in Bayport, the California air was warm as summer.

With their coats slung over their shoulders,

the three detectives hailed a taxi. A short while later, they were dropped off at the elegant Hollywood home of the movie actor.

The house was lit up, and two squad cars were parked in front. Evidently the police were still searching for clues to the kidnappers.

"I don't want you to come in with me," Mr. Hardy said. "Just stay here for now."

Frank and Joe watched their father disappear into the house to discuss the case with police and members of Richard Chase's household.

"Let's take a walk around the block," Joe sugested. "Maybe we'll see something."

Blond-haired and energetic, he was more impetuous than his older brother. He hated the thought of standing there and doing nothing.

"Okay," Frank agreed. "Why not?"

The boys were only halfway down the block when they noticed two men in a parked sedan. In the dark, their faces were barely visible, but they seemed to be watching the sleuths' movements. Frank and Joe tried to appear nonchalant, and walked past the car as if unaware of its occupants.

Suddenly, doors swung open and the two men leaped out, menacing the boys with long knives.

"Get in!" one of them commanded.

Joe gulped. "What do you mean?" he protested nervously. "We haven't done anything. We just—"

"Get in!" the man repeated, motioning with his knife toward the door.

Frank and Joe thought briefly of making a dash down the sidewalk. But the men, both with jet black hair combed straight back, appeared to be professional thugs who would deal with any sudden moves quickly and mercilessly.

"We won't hurt you," the driver said, "unless you try something stupid. We just want to ask you some questions."

The boys could see it would be better to go along with the strangers' demands, so they climbed into the front seat next to the driver. The other thug got into the back and frisked the Hardys for weapons, again warning them not to try anything foolish.

"What were you doing at Richard Chase's house?" the driver asked as he started the car and pulled away from the curb.

"We're fans of his," Frank replied, quickly inventing a story. "We heard on television about his abduction and just came to see this

15

place out of curiosity."

The man in the back seat leaned forward. "I think you're lying!" he hissed.

The boys knew they would have to make up something better to satisfy their captors, and it would have to be soon.

"Okay, okay," Joe confessed. "What we were really hoping was to get acting parts in the film Chase had been working on. We thought maybe the producer or director would be at the house, where we could have a chance to meet him."

The driver chuckled, seeming to believe Joe's explanation. "So you are aspiring young actors, are you?" he said. "And you thought that with Richard Chase out of the picture, there might be need for new talent in the film."

Frank nodded. "If we could only meet the director or the producer, maybe we could talk him into giving us parts. It would be our big break."

"So what are *you* doing here?" Joe nervously challenged the men, trying to turn the questioning around.

"That's none of your business," the man in the back seat growled.

The car was cruising down a wide avenue lined with palm trees. Then the driver turned up a side street and pulled the vehicle to the curb.

"Where are you taking us?" Frank asked apprehensively. In reply, he felt an arm reach over his shoulder and the pressure of a knife blade against his throat!

2 A Nasty Fight

"If you go to the police about this," the thug in the back seat warned, increasing the knife's pressure on Frank's throat, "or if we see you kids nosing around again, we won't be as nice as we were this time. Do you understand?"

Frank and Joe both nodded, relieved that they were being set free. They opened the door and slowly climbed out. The door then was slammed shut and the car drove off.

"Let's report those two to the police," Joe, still shaken from the episode, said angrily.

Frank watched their captors as they went down the street and turned onto the palm-lined avenue. The car was a late model American-made luxury sedan, painted green. Its license plates were obscured by the darkness, making it impossible to read the numbers.

"No," he said finally. "These guys were just hired thugs, who probably won't squeal on the person who hired them. If we go to the authorities, all we'd do is blow our cover."

"You're right," Joe agreed. "Let's go back to the Chase house."

The boys walked through the neighborhood, following what seemed to be the main street. It led past elegant homes, some of which Frank and Joe assumed were owned by wealthy movie people. But the boys got lost and finally went into a gas station with a pay phone.

Frank called Richard Chase's number, hoping his father would still be there. But there was no answer. He then phoned his home in Bayport, hoping that Mr. Hardy had left a message.

"Where have you two been?" came the irritated voice of Aunt Gertrude over the receiver. "Your dad called and said you had disappeared! I knew there would be trouble. I just knew it!"

Frank explained that they had been temporarily sidetracked, and asked his aunt where Mr. Hardy was.

"At the Stars Inn," Aunt Gertrude replied.

"It's somewhere in Hollywood."

"Thanks, Aunty." Frank pressed down the receiver, then got the number for the Stars Inn from Hollywood directory assistance.

"What happened to you?" Mr. Hardy asked anxiously when Frank at last reached him.

"We'll explain later, Dad. Just tell me how to find your hotel." He jotted down the address, then called a taxi.

It was almost three in the morning by the time the boys opened their father's hotel room door. They quickly related their experience, and he agreed it would be better not to report the incident to the police.

"I want you to stick with that story about being actors," he said. "That was a good idea. By the way, I learned that Richard Chase had just returned from filming on location. His family says he was deeply concerned about the movie. His wife had gone shopping late in the afternoon, and when she came home she saw signs of a fight in the house. Her husband was gone."

"Where did the filming take place?" Frank asked.

"In an old hotel near Lake Tahoe," his father replied.

"That's a resort area in the mountains several

hundred miles north of here, isn't it?" Joe asked.

His father nodded. "The hotel is owned by Ian Rider, who is also the producer of the movie. It seems that Rider spends most of his time in San Francisco to take care of the business end of the production. But the cast and crew for *Horror Hotel* are presently staying on location in the mountains."

"Why don't we go up there and check things out?" Frank suggested. "With our cover as aspiring actors already established—"

"That's exactly what I had in mind." Mr. Hardy smiled broadly.

In the morning, the Hardys were awakened by a phone call from Bayport. It was Phil Cohen, a school friend who had often helped the young detectives in solving mysteries.

"I heard you guys are working on the Richard Chase case," Phil said. "Aunt Gertrude told me. Listen, I might be able to help you out."

"How?" Joe, who had answered the phone, asked.

"I have a friend named Tim Adams. He's living right near where Richard Chase was working on his latest film."

"Near Lake Tahoe?"

"That's right," Phil went on. "Tim's been acting as a stunt man in the movie. He's a great skier. It turned out that they needed some skiing scenes so they hired Tim. I called him last night and he told me he knows Chase personally and that he talked with him only a few days ago. Tim wants you guys to come up and see him."

"Great!" Joe exclaimed. "We were heading there anyway. This Tim Adams sounds like he might be able to give us the inside connection we were hoping for! How can we get in touch with him?"

Phil told Joe that Tim was staying at his father's ski chalet, which was located near Lake Tahoe in a resort called Oreville. He gave Joe the chalet's phone number.

"Thanks, Phil," Joe said. He hung up, then dialed the chalet. Tim wasn't home, but his father was.

"Tim is out on the ski slopes today," Mr. Adams said. "I'll be going over there myself soon, and I can tell him to meet you. What time do you think you'll arrive?"

After a brief discussion with Frank and their father, Joe told Mr. Adams that they could be at the Oreville ski area by four o'clock that afternoon.

"Good," Mr. Adams said. "I'll have Tim meet you in the parking lot. He's six feet tall, has light blond hair, and he wears a bright red ski parka with a blue stripe."

Joe thanked Mr. Adams and hung up. "Next question," he said, "is how do we get there."

"There's a car rental agency in the lobby of the hotel," Mr. Hardy said. "You two put on your clothes and I'll go rent you a car."

Half an hour later, the boys were loading their luggage into a dark blue Ford. Mr. Hardy gave them a hand, then said, "The place *Horror Hotel* is being filmed at is called Mountain Hotel. It should be close to the Oreville ski area and Mr. Adams's chalet."

"Tim can fill us in on that," Frank said. "We'll call you as soon as we can."

"I'll be going to San Francisco today, which is the movie producer's base of operation," Mr. Hardy said. "You can reach me at the Rex Hotel."

After saying good-bye, the youths drove off in the Ford. Joe was behind the wheel, while Frank studied a California road map to determine the best route to the Lake Tahoe region. Within a few hours, they were traveling along a narrow highway through the Sierra Mountains.

It was past three o'clock by the time the two boys reached Lake Tahoe. From there, Frank instructed Joe to turn up a road which followed a winding course to the north. Snow covered the mountains, and the air temperature dropped below freezing.

"This is Oreville," Frank said, reading a road sign which marked the outskirts of an old town. He glanced at his watch. "It's almost four, but the ski resort ought to be nearby."

Following signs to the ski area, Joe drove up a steep access road. Within a few minutes, they saw the slopes rising up the side of a mountain. A lodge was set at the base, and the parking lot, where they were to meet Tim Adams, was next to it.

"Hey, look! A snowball fight!" Joe exclaimed with a grin, pointing toward the lodge.

Up ahead, there were ten or more boys of high school age engaged in a fierce snowball battle. One group of about seven outnumbered the other, which seemed to consist of only three. The majority was hiding behind parked cars and pelting the three youngsters with an arsenal of snowballs.

"This looks more like a massacre than a snowball fight!" Frank said with a frown.

"Maybe we should give the underdogs a hand."

As the Hardys drove closer to the scene, they saw that it was, indeed, a serious fight.

"Apparently those three kids were ambushed when they came out of the lodge," Joe said. "See, they dropped their skis. The other boys don't seem to have any equipment and probably hid behind the cars well in advance."

Frank nodded. He watched the trio, which had taken cover in back of a ski rack. However, the rack, which amounted to little more than a one-board fence against which people stood up their skis, offered almost no protection. The three boys were still easy prey for the larger group, who appeared to have an inexhaustible supply of ammunition.

Thinking quickly, Joe swung the car around and brought it to a stop in front of the ski rack, giving the three youths added cover. Then both he and Frank jumped out of the car and started making snowballs of their own.

"Frank! Joe!" a desperate voice called out from behind the ski rack. "You got here just in time!"

The sleuths saw that one of the three boys was tall, blond, and wearing a red parka with a blue stripe.

"Tim!" Frank yelled back. "What's going on here?"

Just then, Joe grabbed his brother's arm and yanked him down. A snowball whizzed over their heads and hit the rack with a loud crack.

"Those aren't snowballs!" Joe gasped. "They're iceballs!"

3 A Horrible Sight

Frank and Joe dropped the snowballs they were making and squatted down next to their car. Clearly, there was nothing funny or friendly about this battle, and the best thing to do would be to get Tim and his two buddies out of the parking lot as soon as possible.

More iceballs flew past the boys, who ducked and dodged to avoid being hit.

"Get in the car!" Frank hissed.

He opened the door of their Ford, and on their hands and knees, Tim and his two friends scurried from behind the ski rack and piled into the back seat. Joe took the wheel again, and Frank sat down next to him.

"Let's go," he urged his brother. "Those iceballs could smash the windows."

Joe put the car into gear. Just then one of the missiles glanced off the windshield. There was no damage, but the boys knew that the side windows were not nearly as thick and could not withstand a similar attack.

The blond detective stepped on the gas and the Ford sped forward. In a moment, they were out of iceball range.

"Thanks for the lift, fellows," Tim Adams said with a sigh of relief. "I wish you'd gotten here a bit earlier, though."

Frank looked over his shoulder at the three passengers in the back seat. Tim had a bad bruise forming where an iceball had clipped him near his left ear. One of the other boys was nursing a bloody nose, and the third one was holding his shoulder in pain.

"Do any of you want to go to the hospital?" Frank asked.

"I'm all right," said the boy with the hurt shoulder. "I don't think I broke anything. It just stings a lot."

Both Tim and the other boy said they were okay, too. They just wanted to go home to clean up their cuts and bruises.

"We'll be glad to take you," Frank offered.

"Thanks," Tim said, then introduced his two friends. The one with the bloody nose was Rick. He was short, and had bushy eyebrows and wavy dark hair.

The other boy was named Paul. He was the same size as Tim, about six feet, with sandy hair and a quick smile. All three looked as if they were fairly well off. They wore brightly colored ski outfits and expensive boots.

"What happened back there?" Joe asked when the introductions were over. "It seems like that bunch had it in for you."

"They did." Tim groaned. "They're the townies."

"Townies?" Frank queried.

"Yes," Tim replied. "That's what we call them. They live in Oreville. We have a longstanding feud going with them. The rich kids against the poor kids, you could say," he concluded with a slight grin.

"It's a pretty rough group to get mixed up with," Joe declared. "It eould get dangerous if you're not careful."

"And it seems as if there are twice as many townies as there are of you," Frank added. "Don't you think it would be better to make a truce?"

"No way!" Paul declared angrily. "Nobody

hurls iceballs at me and gets away with it. They're going to pay for that!"

"There are more than just us three on our side," Tim put in hastily. "We have four other friends who'll fight, and with you two guys we'd outnumber the townies."

"You want us to join your gang?" Joe asked in disbelief.

Tim leaned forward from the back seat. "Sure. As long as you're up here, we could use your help. Phil Cohen said you two were great with your fists, and—"

"Hold on!" Frank exclaimed. "We didn't come up to fight in a local gang war."

"I just thought we could give each other a hand," Tim said defensively. "I may be able to help you with your case, and you could help us take care of those townies. Seems like a good deal to me."

"Talking about our case, how well do you know Richard Chase?" Frank asked. "Phil told us you're a stunt man for the movie."

Tim Adams's face glowed red with embarrassment. "Well, I guess I exaggerated a little," he said. "I only met Chase once when I went out to watch the film being shot at the hotel. And I'm not really a stunt man yet. There are

30

tryouts scheduled for tomorrow, but I stand the best chance of getting the job."

"So you lied to Phil about your involvement with the film just to get us here to help you fight the townies!" Joe exclaimed.

"Well, ah . . ." Tim was clearly uncomfortable. "Yes, I stretched the truth a bit. But I'm sure I can help you. I know where *Horror Hotel* is being filmed, and I know the surrounding area very well. You can stay in my dad's chalet while you're here and borrow ski clothes from us."

"And Tim *is* the best freestyle skier in Oreville," Paul put in. "He'll get the job."

"It's true," Rick added. "Wait till you see him at the tryouts tomorrow. And you saw how tough those townies are. It would be great to have you guys on our side."

The trio in the back seat watched Frank and Joe with pleading expressions.

"I'll tell you what," Frank said finally. "We won't help you fight the townies. Nothing will be solved that way. But we will do our best to put an end to this feud before it gets out of hand."

Tim and his two friends groaned. "You won't be able to," Tim said. "It's been going on

31

forever. Nobody can stop it."

"We'll see," Frank said. He was disappointed that Tim wasn't the connection they had hoped he would be. Now they would have to find another way of penetrating the suspect movie company that Richard Chase had been involved with.

Suddenly Rick called out, "We forgot our skis!"

Joe swung the Ford around and headed back toward the parking lot. There was no sign of the iceball-throwing townies when they arrived. Tim, Rick, and Paul picked up their equipment, which was left scattered outside the lodge.

"I might as well take my car home, too," Paul said. "Rick, I'll give you a ride. This way the Hardys can follow Tim right to the chalet."

"Good idea," Frank said and helped the boys secure their skis to the rack on Paul's car. Tim put his in the back of his station wagon, then drove off with the Ford following close behind.

Mr. Adams's chalet was just off the ski area access road. It was a beautiful, large A-frame house with big glass windows. When the boys had parked the cars, Tim said, "How about some hot cocoa? We have cookies, too."

The Hardys eagerly devoured the refreshments. Then Frank said, "Tim, if you don't mind, I'd like to go to the filming location."

"Not at all," Tim replied, still a bit ashamed of having tricked the boys to visit him. "I'll take you over there. It's only five miles from here."

It was dark when they climbed into the station wagon.

"We were told the hotel is very old," Frank said as Tim drove down the road.

"Not really. It was built ten years ago," their host answered. "But it was designed to look old. It's a really neat place for a horror movie."

On their way, the young people passed through Oreville.

"That's where the townies hang out," Tim said as he pointed to the general store. "There's a room in the back with video games and soda machines. The kids use it as their meeting place."

Frank and Joe looked at the general store and several other buildings, which made up the center of the old town.

"What do people do for a living around here?" Frank inquired.

"Most work in the ski area," Tim replied. "Some are cooks or waiters in the restaurants, others work in slope maintenance, like snow-making and lift operation."

Once they had passed through Oreville, he

drove some distance down the winding mountain road. It was the same route the boys had used coming up from Lake Tahoe earlier. Then he stopped in front of a big, old-looking building. It was set about a hundred feet off the road on the side of a looming, steep hill.

"This is it," Tim announced.

"It *is* perfect for a horror movie," Joe had to admit.

The hotel looked as if it was from another century. It was painted white, had a huge front porch, and was five stories high. Its windows were arched at the top, except for a small round one in the attic. The overall effect was that of an old wooden box, like a dollhouse. Only a few windows were lit.

"We'll go in and see what we find," Frank said. "Tim, why don't you stay here, ready to leave if we have to in a hurry."

"Sure," the Adams boy agreed.

Frank and Joe went to the entrance and knocked. A long while passed until the door suddenly opened all by itself!

The young detectives gasped and backed away. In the hallway, dangling in the air by a rope, was a dead body!

The corpse's eyes stared straight ahead as it swayed slightly. The boys heard an eerie

chuckle from behind the door. Then a man with an impish grin on his face stepped out in front of them. He was thin, in his middle twenties, and upon seeing the visitors' pale faces, he doubled up with laughter.

Frank and Joe were dumbfounded. They weren't sure whether they should grab the man or flee from the hotel, so they just stood there for a moment, gaping.

The young man controlled his laughing. "It's . . . it's just a dummy," he said, gesturing to the corpse. "I made it myself. But your faces were priceless."

Frank and Joe stepped forward to inspect the body more closely. With a sigh of relief, they realized that it must be a prop for the horror movie.

"You sure have a strange sense of humor," Joe said to the man.

"One has to in this business," came the reply. "You see, I'm Bruce, the makeup man for the movie that's being made here. I spend all day producing the most gory, gruesome things. This corpse is one of my masterpieces. Do you like it?"

Joe grimaced. "It sure had me fooled," he said drily.

"Thanks," Bruce said. "Now, what can I do for you two?"

"We're actors," Frank said. "And we heard about the film being shot here. So we thought we'd drive over and find out if you needed any help."

The man shook his head. "You're not the first kids who've come for acting parts. And, as I told the others, we don't need anybody. I'm afraid you've wasted your time."

"We heard about Richard Chase's abduction on television," Frank persisted. "And we thought that with him out of the picture, you might be revising the script to include new characters."

"The director and the writer have started to make some changes," Bruce admitted. "And we may need some new talent when they've finished. We'll be able to use a fat boy for a small role, but neither of you is fat."

Instantly, the same idea crossed the boys' minds. "We have a friend who might fit the bill," Frank said. "We'll send him over."

Bruce shrugged. "Why not?"

The boys said good-bye and left. On their way back to the car, Frank said, "Let's give Chet a call." He was referring to Chet Morton, their chubby best friend in Bayport, who had often accompanied them on assignments. Chet liked to eat more than work, but he could always be relied upon when things got tough.

"He could come out on the first flight in the morning," Joe agreed. "He'd be perfect for the fat role. But he'll . . ."

The young detective was distracted by a man who seemed to be watching them from one of the hotel's second-floor windows. But before Joe could get a good look at him, the lights went out.

"Did you see the guy upstairs?" Joe asked, turning to his brother.

"Who?" Frank looked puzzled.

"There was a man in the window," Joe replied. "He seemed to be watching us."

"I don't see anyone now." Frank shrugged and started to climb into Tim's car.

Suddenly, the front door of the hotel opened and a man dashed out. "Wait a second!" he called and ran down the steps toward them.

4   The Feud

The man stopped in front of the car. "I'm Dutton Foster, the director of the movie," he said. "I overheard you talking to our makeup man and suddenly realized that we may be able to use you after all."

"Oh, great!" Frank said, closely studying the gangly man with bright green eyes and a bushy beard, who seemed about his father's age. He was dressed only in a white cotton shirt and pants and was beginning to shiver from the cold air.

"You mean, you have acting parts for us after all?" Joe asked eagerly.

"No," the bearded man said and shook his

head. "I don't need you to act, but if you want to make some money, I could use you to help move scenery around. We're a bit short of manpower up here."

The boys pretended to be dismayed that they would not be able to act, but inwardly they were more than happy with the offer.

"Does it pay well?" Frank queried, not wanting to appear overeager.

"We pay union rates," the man replied. "Are you interested?"

Frank looked at Joe. "Sure, why not," the younger Hardy said and nodded.

"Give me your names and phone number. I'll call you in a couple of days," the director said.

Tim handed Frank a piece of paper from the glove compartment, and Frank wrote: *Frank and Joe Russell, % Mr. Adams, 377-1778*. Then he handed the note to Dutton Foster, who took it and hurried back into the hotel.

"Was he the man you saw in the window?" Frank asked Joe.

"No. I didn't get a good look at that guy, but he had no beard."

"I wonder if the director's coming outside had something to do with the man in the window," Frank mused.

Joe shrugged. "Let's hope we're hired so we

can get into the place. For all we know, Richard Chase may be tied up in there somewhere."

On the drive back, the Hardys told Tim about their encounter with Bruce, then asked him if they could call their friend Chet from the chalet.

"Sure, be my guest," Tim replied and, once they had arrived, showed them to the phone.

Chet was enthusiastic. "You mean I can be in the movies?" he boomed. "That's the best offer you've made me in a long time!"

"You'd have to be here as soon as possible," Frank told him. "See if you can book a flight to Reno in the morning, then call us back. Reno isn't far from here and we can pick you up."

After he hung up, he looked for their host. "Where's Tim?" he asked Joe.

"He said he had to go on an errand," Joe replied. "But I bet he wants to meet his friends to find a way to get back at the townies."

A few minutes later, Tim's father arrived. Like his son, he was tall and blond. "You must be Frank and Joe Hardy," he said, shaking the boys' hands. Then he sat down on a couch near the fireplace, a worried expression on his face. "Did Tim tell you where he was going?"

"No," Joe said, and filled Mr. Adams in on the iceball fight and their suspicion that Tim and

41

his friends were planning to retaliate.

"I was afraid something like this might happen," Mr. Adams said, bowing his head. "This feud with the Oreville boys is getting out of hand."

"How did it start?" Frank queried.

Tim's father sighed. "It began many years ago, when Oreville was still a mining town. Back then the place was divided into the north and south sides. People who lived on the south side were the miners, and on the north side lived the wealthy mining company owners, among whom was my father."

He stood up and began to pace around the room. "Feelings between the workers and the men who owned and managed the mines were never very friendly," he continued. "But because of certain incidents, including a cave-in when a number of workers were buried alive, the bad feelings erupted into open hostility, with houses burned down and even some gun battles."

"And those feelings still linger on now?" Frank asked, finding it hard to believe that after so many years the bitter mood had not subsided.

Mr. Adams sat down again and shrugged. "The older folks have tried to forget, but the

42

young people still keep the feud alive, as you have seen today with the iceball battle."

"There are no more mines in operation now, are there?" Joe asked.

"No, they were all shut down years ago," the man replied. "The sons of the mine owners, like me, used the land and the money they inherited to build the ski area. This resort is actually located on top of one of the mountains that once was mined."

"Tim calls the boys who attacked him townies," Frank said.

"We used to call them southsiders," Mr. Adams explained. "But they eventually moved all over town, so now they're known as the townies."

"What were the other incidents besides the cave-in that led to bad relations with the miners?" Joe asked.

"I don't really know," Mr. Adams said. "I was very young at the time. But I know the workers were upset with conditions and wages. Now, however, all the townies work for the ski resort and are well paid. Therefore, most of them are content to let bygones be bygones. But some of the kids like to fight, I guess, and they keep the feud alive to give them a reason."

Just then the telephone rang. Mr. Adams

picked it up and then handed it to Frank.

"Hi!" came Chet's voice, loud and excited. "I'll arrive in Reno at nine-thirty in the morning. Can you pick me up?"

"We'll be there," Frank assured him.

A few moments later, Tim and his two friends walked in. All three boys were in even worse shape than they had been after the iceball fight.

"But we got 'em!" Tim announced with a smile, rubbing a new bruise he had acquired right next to the old one.

"Looks as if they got you, too," Joe remarked.

Rick glared at the Hardys. "Well, if you two had come along, we might have finished up looking better than we do." His jacket was torn, and a trickle of dried blood blemished the left corner of his mouth.

"Lay off," Tim warned his friend. "These guys will come around. They just need time."

Not wanting to start an argument, the Hardys kept silent. Mr. Adams, however, wasn't about to drop the matter. "If you boys had any sense," he said heatedly to Tim and his friends, "you'd follow Frank and Joe's example. And I don't want to hear any excuses. This feud of yours has gone just about far enough."

Tim looked hurt. "But the townies attacked

44

us with iceballs, Dad! We can't let them get away with that."

Tim's father leveled a finger at his son. "What's done is done," he said evenly. "But if there's any trouble at the competition tomorrow, I'm going to hold you responsible."

"Competition?" Frank asked.

"Didn't I tell you?" the young skier said. "Tomorrow we're having our annual hotdogging competition. All three of us are entering."

Frank and Joe had seen hotdog skiing competitions on television. The contestants performed different feats of daring on skis, such as flips and spins in the air. The sport required both skill and courage. A number of young skiers had come away from such events with serious injuries.

"Was that what you were talking about when you said you would be trying out for a stunt man part in the film?" Joe queried.

Tim smiled. "Yes. The film company will be shooting the event. The movie they're working on has skiing scenes in it. So they posted notices saying that whoever won the competition would be hired as a stunt man."

Paul winked at Frank and Joe. "Tim's the best. He'll win."

45

Tim beamed. "I hope so. At least I hope that one of us wins. If a townie does, I don't know *what* I'll do."

"The Oreville boys are entering the competition, too?" Frank asked.

"Oh, sure," the young skier answered. "That's what it's all about, us against the townies."

Joe winced. "Aren't you afraid they'll take the opportunity to retaliate?"

"They wouldn't dare," Tim replied, shrugging off the question. "The event would be canceled and they'd probably lose their skiing privileges."

Frank and Joe looked questioningly at Tim's father.

"The hotdogging competition was something I and the other resort owners started a few years back," Mr. Adams explained. "The idea was to give the feuding groups a chance to blow off steam in a healthy, organized way. It's worked well in the past, and the kids love the event. I don't think either group would ruin it by starting a fight."

"And with the chance of getting a part in the movie as a stunt man, all of us will be too busy trying to win," Tim added.

"It seems to me," Frank said seriously, "that in your eagerness to win, you'll be performing more dangerous and daring stunts than ever."

Mr. Adams nodded. "I expect the competition will be fierce tomorrow. But I can't call it off. For one thing, it won't be just the local boys who are competing. Over the years, the contest has grown into a regional event, with skiers coming from all over the West. I can't let them down."

"I can understand that," Joe said.

"What's more," Tim's father went on, "I'm afraid that if we canceled, the feud would get even worse. Aside from the fact that we give the Oreville boys free ski passes, they consider the competition their event. It keeps a lid on the whole thing."

"Don't worry, Dad," Tim said. "The townies don't want to cause trouble any more than we do. And I promise I won't try any stunts I can't handle."

"Good," Mr. Adams said, then went to the kitchen to prepare dinner. Frank and Joe sat around the fire listening to Tim and his friends plan their strategy for the competition. Later, the group retired to the chalet's various bedrooms for a well-deserved rest.

In the morning, the Hardys were up and out the door early to pick up Chet at the airport.

"Looks like snow," Joe remarked, glancing at

an overcast sky as he climbed into the Ford.

"I heard there'd be a storm," his brother said.

They drove through the mountains and arrived at the airport at 9:40. Chet was waiting in the lobby, dressed in a brightly colored shirt and sunglasses.

"You certainly look the part," Frank said and chuckled at Chet's attire. "You're a regular Mr. Movie Star."

Chet raised his eyebrows. "Just because *you* couldn't get the role, don't get envious," he smirked, and put on the yellow down jacket he was carrying over his arm.

The boys headed straight for Oreville. Light snow was falling by now and the film crew was setting up cameras for the hotdogging competition.

Frank and Joe introduced Chet to the director and left them to speak privately. A few minutes later the chubby boy had a smile on his face that quickly changed into an angry scowl when he rejoined the Hardys.

"Did he give you the part?" Joe asked eagerly.

"He did," Chet fumed. "But you guys didn't tell me I only got it because I was *fat*!"

5 *Downhill Race*

Frank and Joe couldn't help but laugh. "It's called typecasting," Frank said. "We were thrilled that they needed someone like you, because to investigate the disappearance of Richard Chase, we've got to have a contact on the inside!"

Chet's anger dissipated as rapidly as it had arisen. "I don't really mind the typecasting," he admitted. "I'm thrilled to have the part. I'm going to start tomorrow."

Since Chet wouldn't be needed until the following day, all three decided to do some skiing. Frank and Joe were both able skiers, but Chet was just a beginner, so he signed up for lessons.

After renting skis, poles, and boots, the boys headed for the slopes. Chet joined a ski class while Frank and Joe moved toward the main chair lift. The snowstorm was now in full swing, with fine flakes falling all over the mountain.

"Do you think they'll have to cancel the competition because of the weather?" Joe asked as they rode up in one of the chair lifts.

"I doubt it," Frank replied. "Visibility on the lower half of the mountain, where the event will take place, is still good."

When they reached the top, however, they were shrouded in a low cloud. They could no longer see the chair in front of them, and they glided through the dense white mist with only a flurry of snowflakes for company.

"It's so quiet, too," Frank said in a hushed tone, enjoying the eerie ride.

Soon the outline of a small cabin appeared ahead of them.

"That's the end of the lift," Frank said. "Are you ready to get off?"

Joe nodded as he watched the lift attendant through a small window. The man seemed bored with his job.

Suddenly Joe's eyes grew wide. "I—I think that's him!" he said excitedly.

The boys were now right in front of the hut and Frank nudged his brother. "Get off!" he called out and the two skied down the ramp leading from the lift to the slopes. "Now, what were you talking about up there?" he asked when they came to a stop.

"I think the lift attendant was the man I saw in the hotel window last night!" Joe exclaimed.

"What!"

"Well, because of the dark I didn't get a good look at him until the last minute, so I couldn't alert you. Did you see him at all?"

"No, I paid no attention to him."

"He was in his early sixties, with thinning gray hair, a narrow face, and sharp cheekbones. But what made him stand out were his sleepy-looking eyes. His eyelids seemed only half open," Joe explained.

"And you're sure it was the same guy?" Frank asked.

"Not completely. His face definitely looked like the one I saw in the window, only . . . only the man last night seemed heavier," Joe concluded with some hesitation.

"Let's talk to him anyway," Frank suggested, and the two boys took off their skis and hiked back up the lift ramp.

The attendant opened the door when he saw them coming. "Something I can do for you?" he asked.

Frank and Joe noticed that he not only had sleepy-looking eyes, but that his teeth were unusually small.

"We went down to the movie site last night to see if we could get acting jobs," Joe began. "I thought I saw you there at one of the upstairs windows. Maybe you have an idea what we can do to work there?"

The attendant shrugged and shook his head, raising his eyelids a fraction. "You made a mistake," he said. "I've been a lift attendant for years and know nothing about the film company. I was home last night. You must've seen someone else."

"I suppose so," Joe said.

"I'm getting cold," the man said and closed the door.

"He really wasn't the same guy," Joe said as they returned to their skis. "He was even skinnier than he appeared through the hut window. It was those eyes that fooled me."

The brothers fastened their bindings, then started off through the falling snow to one of the expert runs. It had been a year since they had skied, but soon they were back in the swing of it.

"This is great!" Joe said gleefully as he stopped at the foot of the first steep incline.

Frank, who had taken the slope a bit more cautiously than his brother, slid to a halt next to Joe. "You said it," he beamed.

They heard shouts coming from above, and then several boys appeared at a crest. They were almost flying over the snow, shouting and whooping as they went.

"Those are the townies!" Joe exclaimed, recognizing the youths from the iceball ambush.

"I know," Frank said. "Let's go."

The Hardys pushed off. By the time the Oreville gang caught up with them, they had already picked up a lot of speed. And then, without a word spoken, they all moved down the hill in an impromptu race!

The Hardys kept up with the wild young men's pace, which soon became as fast as the speed of a car! Neither Frank nor Joe wore goggles, and the falling snow stung their eyes, nearly blinding them. Frank finally gave up the race, but Joe stuck it out, whipping down the mountain at fifty miles an hour!

All of a sudden, the edge of his right ski

caught on a piece of ice. He lost control, but managed to avert a fall. But now he was heading straight for a line of ski-schoolers, Chet among them!

"Watch out!" Joe cried in desperation, but it was too late.

Thwackkkk! He plummeted headlong into the lineup, toppling the novice skiers like dominoes as he went. Luckily, he had been able to slow his pace before the impact, so no one was injured in the collision. But the ski-schoolers were shaken, and slowly got to their feet and brushed the snow from their clothes.

Joe's own fall was spectacular. He tumbled head over heels about fifty feet further down the hill, at last coming to a crashing halt on a level stretch. One of his skis stuck straight up in the snow, the other was half buried in a drift.

The young detective did not move for a few seconds, then he slowly lifted his head to look around.

"Yayyyyy!" a chorus of youthful cheers broke out near him. The townies were applauding him!

"Bravo!" one of the boys shouted. "You were magnificent!"

The group skied up to Joe to help him up. At the same moment, the ski instructor, whose class Joe had disrupted, came down the hill and stopped next to him.

"Are you okay?" he asked.

"I . . . I think so," Joe said. "I hope I didn't hurt anyone else."

"You were lucky you didn't," the man replied gruffly. "And if I ever catch you skiing down the slopes again like a madman, I'll have you removed from this mountain!"

"Yes, sir," Jor answered meekly. "I won't do it again."

The instructor moved on. By now his students had caught up with him and skied past, glaring angrily at the blond boy. Chet pretended not to know the maniac who had collided with them.

"Don't pay any attention to those guys," one of the townies said cheerfully. "They don't know how to have fun. I like your guts."

Joe smiled weakly as the speaker and his friends clustered around him and helped him to his feet.

"I'm Bob," the townie introduced himself when Joe had dusted himself off and put his skis back on. "This is Jay, Fred, Willie, Bret, and Ben."

The boys, who were all in their teens, wore thick sweaters and blue jeans. Bob, who seemed to be the leader, was a husky six-footer with long, curly hair.

"You put up a good race," he said, laughing. "If it wasn't for your spill, you might have beat me."

"Thanks," Joe said. "But don't ask me to do it again. One fall like that is enough."

"Hey," Jay spoke up. "Didn't we see you in the parking lot yesterday?"

Joe nodded. "You were clobbering those other guys, so we thought we'd even up the sides a little."

"I suggest you don't get mixed up in any more fights like that," Bob warned. "It's none of your business."

Joe shrugged. "My brother and I just felt sorry for those fellows."

"Your brother," Bob said. "Is he the guy who quit the race?"

"Right. Here he comes now."

Frank skied up to the group and stopped. "My eyes were killing me," he said. "How'd you manage, Joe?"

"Not too well. I had a bad spill." Joe introduced Frank to the townies, who looked the dark-haired boy over appreciatively.

"You're a good skier," Bob said. "Kept up with the best of us for quite a while. Hey, why don't you two come to the general store about five o'clock? We're going to celebrate our victory after the hotdogging event."

"Sure," Frank said. "See you later."

With that, the townies skied off to get ready for the competition.

"Looks like you made friends with them," Frank said with a grin. "How'd you do it?"

"It wasn't easy," Joe said. "I almost broke my neck!"

6   *The Monster*

Toward the foot of the slope, various jumps were set up in front of the lodge, and a crowd was gathering for the competition. Frank and Joe skied to a point just below the jumps, where most of the spectators were gathered to see the daring stunts close up. The camera crew was ready.

Soon the hotdogging began. The young contestants took turns performing incredible flips and spins as they flew from the ski jumps into the air. Frank and Joe recognized the townies and Tim's friends, all trying to outdo each other in style and degree of difficulty. The judges, who sat in chairs near the jumps, wrote the skiers' scores on cards.

Chet had been trying to find Frank and Joe, and now met up with them. Tim was preparing a double back flip at this point, and the crowd waited expectantly. He waved to his audience, and shouts of "Go, Jolly Jumper!" could be heard.

Then a hush fell over the spectators. The young skier started down the hill, gathering speed for the daring stunt. Suddenly, as he reached the lip of the jump, a shrill scream broke the silence. It sounded inhuman, like the howl of an animal in horrible pain!

"What's that?" Joe blurted, as he saw a man-like creature, covered with hair, appear behind the spectators at the edge of the slope. It had long, sharp teeth dripping with blood!

Tim, having heard the scream and seen the awful creature, lost all concentration as he flew off the jump. What had been intended as a double back flip turned into a wide tumble through the air. Then he hit the slope head first!

The crowd gasped in terror. Panic broke out at the sight of the fall and the hairy, bloody beast. Screaming, the frightened audience began skiing down the hill to get away from the monster.

Joe and Frank set out toward the hideous creature.

"You're not going after that thing!" Chet bellowed in disbelief.

"We have it outnumbered two to one!" Joe called back, even though a knot was forming in his stomach. "Go and look after Tim!"

Chet needed no urging. He skied toward the scene of the accident while Frank and Joe moved into the forest in pursuit of the creature. Soon their way was impeded by dense trees and difficult terrain.

"Take off your skis," Frank panted, already bending down and working on his bindings. But by the time the boys had gotten rid of their equipment, the monster was far ahead of them. However, it had left a trail of footprints in the shape of huge gorilla tracks.

"If that's someone in a monster outfit, which it must be," Joe gulped, "he sure did a good job."

"Right," Frank agreed. "And we have to move fast, otherwise the falling snow will obliterate the tracks."

But they could not walk too well in their ski boots, and soon the prints grew less and less visible as the wind blew powdery flakes into the indentations.

The young detectives hardly saw any trail when they reached the far side of the mountain.

"Maybe we should give up," Joe said, discouraged.

"Just a little further," Frank urged. "Come on, Joe! At least we'll get some idea of the direction the thing is going in."

The prints were almost invisible when the brothers saw them lead into a hole at the side of a cliff.

"This must be the entrance to a cave!" Frank said excitedly. "Look, it's been boarded up, but some of the boards have been torn away!"

"I bet it's an old mine shaft," Joe deduced, remembering what Mr. Adams had told them about Oreville's history as a mining town.

"And whoever was in this outfit knew about it," Frank went on.

The young detectives went inside. But without flashlights, they could not see further than a few feet.

"I think we've reached the end of the trail," Frank whispered as he stared into the darkness of the mine. "Let's hide outside and see if the monster comes out again."

But even though the boys waited until they were shivering from the cold, there was no further sign of the creature.

"I bet there's another exit," Frank said.

Joe nodded. "We'd better head back before we freeze to death."

Their laborious retreat to the slopes warmed the young detectives up again. When they arrived, the competition was still going on and things seemed to be back to normal. Yet, many of the spectators had left.

"Hey, Frank, Joe!" a voice called out. The boys looked up and saw Tim's friend Paul skiing over to meet them. "Did you catch that thing?"

Frank shook his head. "No. We followed its tracks around the mountain, where they disappeared into an old mine shaft. But we couldn't go any further without a light. How's Tim?"

"They took him to the hospital," Paul said gloomily. "He was unconscious and they carried him off on a stretcher. But I called the hospital and the doctor said it wasn't too serious."

"Let's go to the hospital," Frank suggested.

"Okay," Joe said.

"I've talked to the movie director," Paul said when the boys were taking off their skis at the bottom of the mountain. "Someone stole that monster getup—it was to be used in the film. I think it was one of the townies!" he added grimly.

"Why do you think that?" Frank asked.

"Because they wanted to ruin Tim's jump. It's obvious, isn't it? They also know that old mine inside and out. It's one of their favorite haunts. It makes sense that whoever played monster would go there to avoid being caught!"

"Are you sure that the costume was *stolen*?" Frank asked.

"Well, no," the young skier replied. "But I don't see why the movie company would want to hurt Tim. They were going to hire him if he won the contest. It had to be the townies."

"Let's talk to the director before we drive to the hospital," Frank said.

"I have an errand to run," Paul announced. "See you later."

Before he left, Joe asked him one more question. "Who is that chair lift attendant at the top of the main lift?"

"That's Ray Hodges," Paul replied. "He's been working here ever since the place opened. Lived his whole life in Oreville."

"So he was around when Oreville was still a mining town?"

"Yes, why?"

"Just curious. He's a strange-looking man," Joe commented.

"I thought you realized he wasn't the man you saw in the window yesterday," Frank said to his brother after Paul had parted from them.

"I know," Joe replied. "But he had the same funny eyes, so I was curious."

The film crew was still set up at the bottom of the slope, and the bearded director was there along with the cameraman, the sound man, and several technicians.

When Mr. Foster saw them, he waved, recognizing them from the night before. "I was going to call you boys," he said. "We'll be needing you at the hotel tonight to rearrange some sets."

"Good. We'll be there," Frank promised. "But now we'd like to talk to you about something else. That boy who was hurt in the competition is a friend of ours. And we've been told that the monster that caused the accident wore one of your costumes."

The director nodded. "I'm sorry about what happened. I called the hotel right after the fall because I recognized the costume. One of my men told me that some kid had broken into the back door and stolen the outfit."

"Did you get the incident on film?" Frank inquired.

"My cameraman thinks he caught it, monster and all," the director answered, breaking into a big grin.

"Do you mind if we take a look at it?" Joe pressed.

"Sure you can see it. We'll be sending the film to our lab in San Francisco for developing. But we should have it back by tomorrow night."

The bearded director's grin widened even more. "I'm thinking about using the scene in the movie. It was very dramatic. If we do use it, I'd like your friend to act in a number of fill-in scenes."

"We'll tell him," Frank said. "It'll make him feel better."

"We're on our way to the hospital now," Joe added. "Would you mind if we stopped by the hotel and took a look at the wardrobe department? Maybe one of the people there can give us a clue as to who was responsible." He was also hoping that they might find a clue to Richard Chase, but he did not mention that.

The director shrugged. "Why don't you wait till tonight, when you'll be there anyway?"

Joe had wanted to look around while the film crew wasn't there, but he agreed.

Just then, Tim's friends Paul and Rick skied up.

"We're on our way to have it out with the townies," Rick announced. "Are you two with us or not?"

7 *The Strange Hotel*

Frank and Joe looked at the angry boys. They could see Tim's friends were ready for action and would be difficult to restrain.

"We're going to see Tim at the hospital," Joe said. "Why don't you guys come along?"

"He's okay," Rick said. "I talked to him on the phone. He has a mild concussion and a sprained ankle. But he could've been killed in that fall! We'll visit him later. First we'll take care of the townies."

"So," Paul challenged. "Are you with us or not?"

"We told you before," Frank snapped. "We

won't get involved in this feud as your bullies. We don't even know whether the townies were responsible for the accident."

"What are you talking about?" Paul cried. "You told me yourself that you followed the monster to the mine shaft, and we all know the townies have played there since they were kids!"

Frank glanced at the film director, who was following the conversation with great interest. "Let's talk this over in the parking lot," he said quietly to his friends.

Once the boys were standing at the Hardys' car, Frank continued. "Look, something about this whole setup bothers me. If the townies wanted to remove Tim from the competition, they could have done it in a much more subtle way, without drawing such obvious suspicion to themselves."

"But who else would have had a motive?" Rick demanded.

"I don't know," Frank said. "But we're going to find out!"

"Well," Paul acceded, "you two are supposed to be such hotshot detectives. We'll give you a chance to prove the townies are innocent before we cream them."

"Thanks," Frank said with relief. "Now let's all go to the hospital. I'm sure Tim would like company."

The boys piled into the Ford and reached the medical center before visiting hours were over.

Tim Adams was in good spirits and happy to see his friends. He was especially pleased to learn that the film director was thinking of using him in the horror movie after all. He had suffered only a mild concussion, and his left leg was bandaged.

"They tell me I'll be out of here tomorrow," he said. "Then I have to take it easy for a few days until my headache goes away."

Just then Mr. Adams and Chet walked in, and, after greetings all around, settled themselves into two folding chairs.

"I don't know why the Oreville boys would do such a thing," Tim's father said sadly. "Now I'll have to call off the competition altogether for the next year, as well as revoke their skiing passes. The only reason we didn't stop the contest today was because we were afraid it would erupt into a full-scale battle if we did."

"Don't be too hasty," Frank advised. "Someone else might have staged this whole thing, perhaps even the film company. The director was very eager to use the scene in his movie."

"I can't believe that," Tim said. "You just told me they're planning to give me a part. And the director sounds like a very nice person to me."

"You never know," Frank stated. Then the Hardys said good-bye to Tim and the others and drove to Oreville to meet the townies at the general store.

It was quite large, with a soda counter and a game room in back, where the townies were already gathered.

But there was no celebration. The boys stood around gloomily with other friends. There were a few girls among the crowd, one of whom, named Lise, was particularly attractive.

"What's the matter, didn't you win anything?" Joe asked.

"Actually, I did end up winning the contest," Bob said.

"So why the sour faces? This'll get you a part in the movie!"

Bob shook his head. "If I get it, I'll let that guy who took the spill, Tim Adams, have it."

Frank and Joe looked surprised.

"That's very nice of you," Frank said. "But it wasn't your fault that Tim Adams fell."

"No, it wasn't," Bob agreed. "But he's the son of one of the resort owners. He's also one of the guys we're feuding against. Now they all think we did that monster prank to get the movie part. We'll have our ski passes canceled and they'll probably stop the hotdogging competition forever."

"Maybe by letting Tim have the movie part," Ben put in, "we can convince people we had nothing to do with the accident."

Frank nodded. "Yes, it's a good idea to make the offer, even though the director is already planning to use Tim in the movie."

"How do you know none of your friends were involved in the monster affair?" Joe questioned.

"None of us would've pulled a stunt like that!" Bob declared with conviction. "It's just that after years of fighting and the snowball attack the other day nobody will believe us."

"We followed that phony creature around the mountain to an old mine shaft," Joe went on. "And we heard that you guys used to hang out in those mines."

"Now *you're* suspicious of us, too, aren't you?" Willie cried out angrily. "I tell you, somebody wanted to frame us, that's what it was. Adams and his friends set it all up so we would lose our ski passes!"

"Don't be silly," Frank said. "He wouldn't risk his life for something like that."

Willie's anger subsided. "I guess you're right."

"But," Frank went on, "I do believe someone was trying to frame you. But it wasn't the guys you're fighting with. It must be someone else!"

Joe nodded. "Why don't you help us find out who did it?"

The Oreville boys eagerly volunteered. "But how are we going to do that?" Jay asked.

"We'll meet here tomorrow," Frank decided. "Meanwhile, try to think who could have a motive for either injuring Tim Adams or hurting you because of it. Also, I'd advise you to lie low in case his friends are planning to retaliate."

The townies agreed; then the Hardys left the general store and drove to the Mountain Hotel.

Frank knocked on the door, half expecting to be met with another of the makeup artist's gruesome scenes. But this time, it was opened quickly by the bearded director, who let the boys in. "The set designer will be down shortly and tell you what to do. We'll need you to help with a set in the cellar."

With that, Foster left them standing in the hall and went through an archway into the hotel

73

lobby. Several people were sitting there in armchairs, going over the film script and discussing the next day's shooting schedule. Frank and Joe studied their faces. They seemed to be a mixture of actors and crew. The man whom Joe had seen in the second floor window was not among them.

Then the boys' gaze wandered around the interior of the hotel. It was ornately decorated, with moose heads and a grizzly bear head hanging from the walls. Thickly stuffed chairs, elaborately designed old rugs, and a collection of old vases and figurines on shelves gave the place a turn-of-the-century look.

"You must be the two boys who came to help with the set," said a man who descended the stairs into the hall. He was even heavier than Chet.

"Yes," Frank said. "We're Frank and Joe Russell."

"My name's Ernest DeZao," the set designer said. "Follow me."

As he led the young detectives down a flight of stairs into the basement, Joe said. "What's this movie all about?"

"Just another scary film for the kids," the fat man answered. "It's the story of a scientist who comes to stay at this remote hotel to finish an experiment. It gets out of control, and the scientist slowly turns into a bloodthirsty monster which then starts killing the hotel guests."

"We saw the crew at the ski lodge today, Frank went on. "What did that have to do with the film?"

"Well," Ernest replied, "the monster is finally trapped in the basement, but it escapes out the window. In the original script, it was tracked down in the woods. But since Richard Chase, the main star, was abducted the other day, Dutton has been making some changes to include the skiing competition."

"Was the stolen outfit the costume for the film's monster?" Joe asked.

"Yes, it was," Ernest confirmed. "But we keep extra costumes handy, so we won't miss production tomorrow."

They had arrived in the basement and Ernest pointed. "This is supposed to be a storage room for the hotel," he said. "I need you to pile a bunch of furniture into the room. You'll have to get it from upstairs."

For the following hour, Frank and Joe gathered couches, chairs, and tables from all over the hotel and took them to the cellar. They also used the opportunity to search for the missing actor, but there was no sign of him.

They were carrying a couch along the second-floor hallway, when Frank said, "Shh! Listen."

The boys set the couch down as they heard the director's voice from behind one of the closed doors. It sounded as though he was talking to somebody on the telephone.

"We'll have a truck deliver the film by ten in the morning," Dutton said. "Can you have the rushes developed by tomorrow afternoon? Okay—hold on a second."

Hearing footsteps coming toward the door, Frank and Joe quickly picked up the couch.

The door flew open and Dutton Foster confronted them. "What are you kids doing here?" he demanded.

"We're getting furniture to put in the basement," Frank said, acting surprised at the question. "The set designer told us—"

"All right, all right," the director said irritably. "Then get on with it."

He watched the boys carry the couch to the stairs before returning to the room.

"He seemed pretty touchy," Joe whispered.

Frank nodded. "As if he were afraid to be overheard."

Having caught only a snatch of the director's conversation, the Hardys didn't know what to make of it. They deduced, however, that he had been talking about taking the rushes, meaning the film that was shot that day, to the lab in San Francisco for developing.

"I wonder why they need a truck," Joe said, still in a low tone. "A car would be cheaper and faster."

"Maybe they're planning to transport other things," Frank suggested.

"Hey, boys!" a voice called out suddenly. "When you're finished with that load, come to the top floor."

Frank and Joe glanced up a flight of stairs to see Bruce, the makeup artist.

"I want you to carry something down for me," Bruce explained.

"Okay," Frank said.

Once they deposited the couch in the cellar, they climbed to the attic. A wooden door was at the end of a narrow, steep flight of stairs. Frank opened it and went inside, then backed away with a stifled scream.

On the floor lay Bruce in a pool of blood, with a long sword stuck through his neck!

8 *The Accident*

After their initial shock, the boys rushed toward the man. Then Joe saw Bruce wink.

"I think we just came across another display of Bruce's sense of humor," the young detective said sourly.

Bruce sat up. "Pretty good, eh?" He laughed as he detached the trick sword.

"You called us here for that?" Frank sounded angry.

"No," Bruce said. "I'd like you to take this bureau out of here and put it in the basement."

The bureau was as tall as the boys and weighed over a hundred pounds. Frank and Joe hoisted it up carefully and carried it down the steep stairs.

"I wish they'd put an elevator in this place!" Joe groaned as they maneuvered the heavy object to the top of the fourth-floor stairway.

"I suppose the producer wanted it to be authentic," Frank said. "Remember, Tim told us he owns the place."

The boys started down the stairs with Joe in the lead. But they hadn't descended more than a few steps when he suddenly lost his footing!

"Aaaaeeee!" the blond detective cried out as he fell backward. He let go of the bureau and tumbled headlong down the stairs.

Frank tried for a moment to hold on to the heavy piece of furniture so it would not crash down on his brother. But he lost his grip and the bureau rolled toward Joe, who lay at the bottom, dazed from his fall!

Just in time, though, he looked up and rolled out of its path.

Frank flew down the stairs. "Are you okay?" he asked.

"I . . . I think so," came the hesitating answer. "But the bureau got wrecked." Joe pointed to scattered pieces of wood around him.

"I'm sure glad you got out of the way of that thing," Frank said. "Did you trip on the stairs?"

Joe knitted his brow. "I was very careful," he said. "I believe my foot caught on something."

Both boys looked up the stairs to see if there was anything that could have caused Joe to trip. All they saw, however, was the makeup artist, who stood at the top of the landing and looked down.

"Is anybody hurt?" he asked worriedly.

"Not really," Joe said. "But I'm sure I'll have a few bruises."

Bruce laughed in relief. "And I figured I was the only guy around here who made scary scenes!"

Frank looked at him suspiciously, but kept his thoughts to himself. "Sorry about the bureau," he apologized.

"Don't worry about it," Bruce advised. "But I think you should be a bit more careful from now on. Strange things happen around here to people who aren't careful!"

His last words had a hint of threat in them. Both boys wondered if his talents included causing accidents—such as stringing a wire across the stairway when nobody was looking!

By now several members of the film crew had rushed to the scene from below. Among them was the director.

"I think you two have done enough damage for today," he grumbled. "Why don't you go home. I'll have your paychecks sent to you."

The boys nodded meekly and went to wash up. Afterward they checked the stairs for hidden wires but found none. If the makeup artist had caused the accident, he had removed the evidence!

Next, the Hardys looked for Bruce. "I hear your monster costume was stolen from the hotel today," Frank said. "It caused our friend Tim Adams to fall. What do you know about it?"

"Nothing," Bruce replied. "When I came back to the hotel after lunch, the back door was open and the outfit was missing. Some fake blood had been stolen, too."

"Had the door been unlocked?" Joe asked.

"No. The latch was broken on the outside. Here, I'll show you." Bruce led the young detectives to the rear entrance. "I guess some kid broke in," he declared.

"Why a kid?" Joe inquired.

"I heard there was a feud going on between two teenage gangs in the area. Maybe it had something to do with that."

"I didn't see you at the slopes today," Frank said casually. "Weren't you needed?"

"Well . . . I was back and forth," Bruce answered uneasily. Then his expression turned sharp. "What are you guys getting at?"

"Oh, nothing," Frank said. "We just didn't

81

like our friend getting hurt because of that stupid prank and we're trying to find out who was behind it. I thought maybe you saw somebody suspicious around, that's all."

"I suggest you talk to those kids!" the makeup artist shouted. "They might have an answer for you." With that, he stormed away, and the boys left the hotel.

"Let's take a look at the trucks," Frank suggested as he closed the door behind them.

Joe nodded, and the Hardys circled around the hotel. Two equipment trucks were parked in the back. Joe tried opening the rear doors, but they were locked. The boys jotted down the license numbers, then returned to the Adams chalet.

They found Tim's father and Chet sitting in front of a crackling fire. Frank told them what had happened and concluded with the announcement that they would drive to San Francisco the next day.

"The film director was very secretive," Joe added. "We think they're up to something."

"What am I supposed to do all by myself?" Chet demanded.

"Just go to the hotel as planned," Frank advised. "And keep your eyes and ears open."

Then the Hardys called their father in San

Francisco. "I'm glad to hear from you," Mr. Hardy said. "I want you to check something for me."

"Sure, Dad," Frank said. "What is it?"

"In a side compartment of Richard Chase's suitcase I found a piece of paper with my name on it," the detective replied. "The stationery is very old, almost brown with age, and the letterhead says Grizzly Bear Lodge. Above the name is a drawing of some mountains and pine trees. Chase must've picked it up when he was near Lake Tahoe, and I want you to look into it."

"Can we do that later?" Frank asked and told his father that they wanted to follow the truck.

"Okay," Fenton Hardy said. "Also, tell Chet to be on the lookout for the stationery. It could be an important clue."

"Do you know the name of the lab the film company is using, Dad?" Frank asked.

"Yes. Werner Laboratories on Spring Street," Mr. Hardy said.

After Frank hung up, he asked Mr. Adams if he had ever heard of Grizzly Bear Lodge.

"No," Tim's father said. "Is it supposed to be around here?"

"I don't know, but I'd like to check the phone book," Frank said.

To the boys' disappointment, there was no listing under that name. "We'll have to look into it when we get back," Joe declared. "Now we'd better get some rest. We have to get up early."

Assuming that the truck would not go straight to the lab, the Hardys felt it would be leaving early. In order not to miss it, they stationed themselves in front of the hotel very early the next morning when it was still dark outside and waited. There wasn't a single light on in the hotel, and no sign of life.

"Maybe we should look around back to see if both trucks are still there," Joe suggested, and volunteered to go. After a few minutes, he returned, dismayed.

"One of the trucks is gone!" he said. "We missed it!"

9 *Mysterious Cargo*

Frank bit his lip. "That's too bad," he said. "But let's go anyway. We know the address of the lab. Maybe we can catch up with the truck there."

The boys stopped for breakfast on the way and arrived at the lab shortly before ten. They did not have long to wait before the truck pulled up in front of the building.

"Should we talk to the guy?" Joe asked and pointed to the driver, who was climbing out of the cab carrying large cans of film.

"No, let's hold off," Frank suggested.

The driver went inside and returned a few minutes later after having dropped off the undeveloped film. He got back into his truck and drove off. Frank and Joe followed at a safe distance. Soon the truck entered a warehouse district and stopped in front of the loading dock of a large building. Two men came out and helped the driver unload several crates.

Frank and Joe were watching from a distance. "Those boxes are very heavy," Frank pointed out, noticing that the muscular men were straining under the weight. "Maybe that's why the truck left the hotel in the middle of the night, to pick up those crates."

"Let's see if we can get a closer look," Joe suggested, and the two left their car and cautiously approached the warehouse on foot. By circling around the place, they found a good vantage point at the far corner of the building, where they could conceal themselves.

Suddenly, Frank felt a sharp steel point against his back!

"Aspiring actors, huh?" a harsh male voice growled.

Frank looked over his shoulder to see the two men who had threatened them in the car during their night in Hollywood! Both men wore sunglasses and carried the long knives they'd had with them before.

"I knew you guys were up to no good," one of the thugs said. "I warned you two once before, but I suppose you didn't take me seriously. In any case, you're not getting away this time!"

"What do you want?" Joe demanded.

"Get in the car!" The thug pointed to the familiar green sedan.

He followed the boys, his weapon poised, while his crony ran to the warehouse, apparently planning to notify the truck driver.

Frank slid into the back seat of the sedan.

Joe climbed in next, and the thug started to move in beside him. Just then, Joe made a half turn and grabbed their attacker's wrist that held the knife. In the same motion, he yanked the man's arm into the car and slammed the door shut on it!

"Yowwww!" the thug screamed as the heavy car door caught him painfully above the elbow. He lost his grip on the knife and dropped it inside the car when he withdrew his injured arm. Joe closed the door.

Before the other man could rush back to the scene, Frank dove into the front seat and locked both doors. Then he looked at the ignition.

"I'm glad they left the keys in the car," he murmured as he started the engine. The two men, meanwhile, were looking for objects to break the windows.

"Hurry up!" Joe urged, seeing one of their attackers picking up a steel pipe.

The car jerked forward, and within a few seconds the boys were driving down the street. They pulled up behind their Ford, changed cars, and tossed the green sedan's ignition keys into a sewer drain.

"That'll keep those guys from following us until we can get away!" Frank said gleefully.

Joe threw the knife after the keys. "Right," he said. "Now let's get out of here."

Once they were in the downtown area, they called Mr. Hardy and arranged to meet him in a health food restaurant. Soon, all three detectives were together again and comparing notes on the case.

After hearing the boys' story, Fenton Hardy drummed his fingers on the table. "It's beginning to make some sense," he said. "I've checked into Rider and his company's finances, and there's an element of shadiness about his accounting practices. Furthermore, one of the horror movie's financial backers is a group of investors who have put money in other projects of questionable nature. What you saw at the warehouse today may tie in with that. I'll notify the police and see that they have the place watched."

"Good idea," Frank agreed.

"Now look what I've got for you here," Mr. Hardy said as he pulled a piece of paper from his pocket. He unfolded it and handed it to his sons.

"That's the stationery you mentioned over the phone," Joe said. "From the Grizzly Bear Lodge."

"Right," Mr. Hardy replied. "Chet called me from the Mountain Hotel about an hour ago. While they were setting up today's scenes, he found a whole pad of the stationery on a desk. When he asked what it was for, he was told it was a prop for the movie."

"You mean Grizzly Bear Lodge is the fictitious name given to Mountain Hotel for the film?" Joe asked.

Mr. Hardy nodded. "Yes. And in that case, you'd think the stationery would have been printed recently."

"But it looks so old!" Frank objected.

"That's the mystery," Mr. Hardy agreed. "I think Richard Chase brought a sheet back home with him to show it to me. It must be an important clue. But what does it mean?"

"Maybe there really is a Grizzly Bear Lodge somewhere," Joe suggested. "And maybe Chase is there."

Mr. Hardy shook his head. "I've checked this whole area, and there is no such place."

"Suppose there was one, but it's no longer in existence," Frank ventured.

"That's my theory, too," Mr. Hardy agreed. "This could be leftover writing paper from an old hotel by this name."

"But why would they use it in the film?" Joe asked.

Mr. Hardy shrugged. "I don't know. The scriptwriter lives here in town, and it might be well worthwhile to pay him a visit!"

"Let's go right after lunch," Frank said.

Soon they were driving along a crowded highway toward a fashionable residential suburb near the beach, and finally stopped in front of a modern high-rise apartment building.

"You boys might as well wait for me here," Mr. Hardy said. "No need for all three of us to go up."

The young detectives agreed, and their father went inside. He returned in less than five minutes.

"What happened, Dad?" Joe asked. "Was the scriptwriter out?"

"No," Mr. Hardy said as he climbed into the car. "I talked to him."

"Well, what did he say?" Frank said eagerly.

"He told me that the script was altered considerably after he handed it in. He never used the name Grizzly Bear Lodge!"

10 A Planned Crash

Frank and Joe looked disappointed.

"Did he know about a hotel called Grizzly Bear Lodge?" Frank asked.

The detective shook his head. "Never heard the name in his life."

Joe sighed. "So where do we go from here?"

"I suggest you drop me off and head back to Oreville," Mr. Hardy told the boys. "The answer to our puzzle may well lie at the filming location. But be careful. The film company knows by now your real motives for being there."

"Okay, Dad," Frank said. "But I do want to stop off at the film lab. Those rushes are probably developed by now, and the truck may pick them up."

The young sleuths dropped their father off at the Rex Hotel, then went to Werner Laboratories.

The man behind the counter shook his head when they asked about the rushes. "No, they're still here. We just finished developing them a little while ago. Are you involved with the movie?"

"A friend of ours is acting in it," Frank answered. "We were hoping to have a look at them to see how they came out."

"Well, the producer is in the screening room reviewing the film right now," the man said. "Why don't you join him? I'll show you the way."

This was more than the boys had hoped for! They could meet the producer, Ian Rider, and also see the results of the ski scene. Eagerly they followed the clerk down a hallway into a room.

It was dark except for the flicker of the film. On a large screen, they saw one of the boys go down the ramp, make a full twist, then land successfully at the base of the jump.

"Who are you?" a gruff voice demanded from a chair some distance away from them.

"We've been helping with the production," Joe answered, barely able to make out the man's features. "We were in town and stopped by to ask if the rushes were ready. We'd really like to see how they came out."

"I don't remember hiring you boys," the man said suspiciously.

"Mr. Foster hired us on location in Oreville," Joe explained.

"Okay then. Sit down," Mr. Rider said tersely, then turned to watch the movie again.

The Hardys took seats in back of the screening room and watched the various competitors as they performed their hotdogging stunts. All shots were framed similarly to show the jump as the skiers flew into the air.

Then, for some reason, the camera angle pulled wider and shifted to the left, focusing on the edge of the woods. Then Tim appeared on the right, flying down the jump.

Suddenly, at the left side of the picture, the hairy monster came running out of the woods, and emitted its howl, confusing the crowd and foiling Tim's jump!

Frank and Joe winced as they watched their friend tumble and land on his head in the snow. As people panicked, the monster disappeared into the woods again and the rushes were finished.

"Re-run that last scene," the producer said over a phone to the projectionist.

The screen went dark for a moment as the film was rewound. Then the monster scene was repeated.

Frank leaned over and whispered in his brother's ear. "Did you see the way they shifted the camera before Tim's fall?"

Joe nodded. "As if they knew exactly what would happen!"

"Right. That monster stunt was deliberately staged for the movie!"

Suddenly, the lights came on. Ian Rider stood up and prepared to leave. He was fairly short, a little overweight, and had a receding hairline. But what distinguished him was a pair of sleepy-looking eyes, just like the eyes of the chair lift operator!

He glanced briefly at Frank and Joe, then left the screening room without a word.

"That's the man in the window!" Joe said, excitedly gripping his older brother's arm.

"You said the same thing about Ray Hodges," Frank reminded him. "Are you sure this time?"

"Positive. And you know what? I bet those

two are related. Rider is heavier than Hodges, but their faces are similar, and those eyes are identical. Anyway, I want to talk to Rider."

Uncertain about his brother's decision to confront the producer, Frank nevertheless followed Joe down the corridor in pursuit of the man. They caught up with him outside as he was about to get into his car.

"Hi!" Joe said with a friendly smile, trying to appear casual. "We just wanted to thank you for letting us sit in on the screening."

"No problem," the man said with a thin smile and began to close the door.

"That's a pretty nice place you have up near Oreville," Joe stalled, referring to the Mountain Hotel.

"I'm glad you like it," Rider commented, his growing irritation showing.

Joe leaned against the car door in such a way that the producer couldn't close it without being rude. "Do you come from around here?" he asked.

"No!" Rider snapped. "Now if you'll excuse me, I'll—"

"Do you have any relatives who live in Oreville, like a cousin?" Joe persisted.

"No, I don't! Now I really must be going."

With that, Rider pushed Joe from the door and closed it. Then he drove off.

"I'm not sure that was such a great idea," Frank said as he watched the producer disappear in traffic.

Joe shrugged. "Our covers are blown anyway," he said. "And we did find out one thing. Rider's lying."

"You can't be sure of that," Frank cautioned.

"Do you have any doubts?"

Frank shrugged. "He certainly has the same eyes and the same small teeth that Hodges has," he said thoughtfully.

"Right. Now, shall we wait for the truck or go back?"

"I suggest we return to Oreville. As Dad said, the answer to the mystery probably lies at the movie site."

It was quite late when the boys passed through the village on their way to the Adams chalet. A cold wind was blowing, and snowdrifts were beginning to pile up along the sides of the buildings. The general store was dark.

They had just about passed the townies' meeting place, when Frank said, "Wait a minute. Let's go back there. I think I saw something."

"What?" Joe asked and put the car in reverse.

"I don't really know. A flicker, maybe a flashlight," Frank said. "It was very faint."

The boys parked the car and climbed out. They walked to the window and peered into the dark store. Indeed, a faint shimmer of light came from inside.

"Do you think someone's in there?" Joe whispered.

Frank shrugged. "It could be a night light," he deduced. "Only . . . it seemed to move before."

As quietly as possible, Joe tried to open the door, but it was locked. Not a sound came from inside.

After the boys had stood there for a few minutes, Joe began to shiver with the cold. "It's nothing," he said. "Let's go."

He was about to turn around when Frank grabbed his arm. "Wait a minute," the older Hardy whispered. "I smell something." He leaned down and sniffed the air at the bottom of the door. "Joe! It's gas!"

11 Sabotage Attempt

Joe crouched down next to his brother. Indeed, a faintly acrid odor filled his nostrils. "You're right!" he exclaimed. "It's gas. The store must be full of it! Somebody left the stove on!"

"We have to get in and turn it off," Frank said. "All it would need is one lit match to blow the place sky high!"

"But we can't just break in!" Joe objected.

"There's no time for anything else," Frank said. "This is an emergency!" He picked up a rock and smashed the window next to the door. Then he reached through the broken pane and unlatched the door from the inside.

The boys took deep breaths to avoid inhaling

the fumes, and rushed in. "Open all the windows," Frank commanded. "I'll get the stove." With that, he ran to the soda counter in the back of the store.

Sure enough, the gas burners of the stove had all been turned on, allowing the explosive gas to collect in the room.

Frank quickly shut off the burners and was about to run to the door for more air when he noticed that the room was lit with a candle, not a night-light. The candle was perched on top of the refrigerator. With his last breath, he blew out the flame, then dashed for the door.

"Did you turn off the stove?" Joe asked when he joined his brother outside a moment later. He coughed as he spoke, having inhaled some of the gas.

Frank took a large gulp of fresh air before answering. "Yes," he said at last. "And it looks as if it was attempted sabotage. We were lucky to get out of there alive!" He told Joe what he had found.

Joe was silent, shivering over their close call. Both boys knew that the leaking gas was heavier than air, and had sunk to the floor at first. Then, as more of the gas collected, it would have risen until it reached the burning

candle on the refrigerator. At that point, the store would have exploded.

"Good thing the gas level wasn't up to the candle yet," Joe said. "Otherwise we'd have been blown to bits!"

Frank nodded. "Well, everything's okay now. But we'd better call the police."

"They'll blame it on Tim's friends," Joe cautioned. "They're the ones with a clear motive for wanting to sabotage the townies' hangout."

"Do you think they actually did it?"

Joe shook his head. "I can't believe that! Whoever staged the monster stunt did it!"

Frank nodded. "But we have to notify the authorities," he insisted. "After all, we broke into the place." He called from a pay phone in the store, and then the boys turned on all the lights to look for clues.

"Here's how the saboteur got in," Joe said, finding a side window which had been pried open.

"And here come the police," Frank said.

A patrol car stopped outside and an officer stepped out. He had a youthful, well-scrubbed appearance. "I'm Sergeant Baker," he said, and thanked the boys for their quick action.

As they had supposed, the young sergeant was well aware of the feud between the Oreville boys and Tim's friends, and he planned to question Tim and his buddies the next morning. After taking down a report on the incident, Baker searched the store himself. But aside from the pried-open window, he found nothing. Taking the candle as evidence, he left.

"Let's talk to Tim," Frank said. "This thing is getting out of hand."

The Hardys drove to the Adams chalet. Mr. Adams opened the door for them, his eyes sleepy. He was dressed in a robe.

"Sorry to wake you up," Frank apologized.

"That's okay," Tim's father yawned. "Come in."

"We'd like to talk to Tim," Joe said.

"He's asleep. Can't you wait till morning?"

"Not really. It's important."

Reluctantly, Mr. Adams showed Frank and Joe to his son's room. The boys turned on the light and shook the sleeping boy, who groggily came to his senses.

"What's the matter?" he asked.

"Something quite serious," Frank said as he settled himself at the edge of Tim's bed. Then he and Joe told about the sabotage attempt.

"You realize who's going to be blamed," Joe concluded.

"My friends wouldn't do anything like that!" Tim protested, now wide awake. "That's a serious crime!"

"We think so, too," Frank admitted. "Especially after we saw the rushes of yesterday's filming." He explained what they had noticed, and Tim gritted his teeth.

"It's incredible!" he fumed. "If it really was the movie company who did this just to get a good shot of the accident, why . . . that's attempted murder! I could've broken my neck in that spill!"

"Yes," Frank said. "But so far we're not sure exactly who did it and why. Meanwhile, why don't you guys get together with the townies and put an end to your feud?"

Tim sighed and rolled his eyes. "Listen," he said. "The fighting has been going on for a long time, and I'm not in command of my friends."

"You could try to persuade them," Joe insisted. "At least make a truce until everything is cleared up."

"I'll do my best," Tim promised.

"Good," Frank said. "I have a feeling that something more than your accident and those film scenes are involved here, and we have to get to the bottom of this."

Just then Chet entered Tim's bedroom, having been awakened by the noise. "So you guys are back," he said, rubbing his eyes. "What did you find out?"

"Plenty," Joe said and told Chet what had happened.

"Wow!" Chet said when his friend had finished. "That's hard to believe!"

Joe nodded. "What about you?" he asked. "Have you learned anything today?"

"The director had me running around in the woods most of the time," Chet replied. "They were filming a scene of me being chased by the monster. It was exhausting. But I did get a copy of the script. I thought you might like to see it."

Chet went to his room and returned a few moments later with a folder. Although tired, Frank and Joe spent the next hour reading every page. The story did not include Tim's accident, but it was clear that Richard Chase's disappearance required changes in the script.

"Do you have to work tomorrow?" Frank asked Chet when he was finished.

"Yes. The director wants to get some close-up shots in the morning."

"See if you can find the revised version of this script," Frank said. "It may be important."

"I'll try," Chet promised. Then all the boys went to bed, too tired to discuss the case any more.

The next morning, Frank and Joe drove to Oreville to question people about the name Grizzly Bear Lodge. After talking to various residents without results, they met a man with white hair and steely blue eyes, who was shoveling his driveway. He seemed to have an accurate memory of Oreville's history.

"Sure," he replied to the young detectives' inquiry about Grizzly Bear Lodge. "There was a place by that name around here. But it burned down about fifty years ago. If you'll wait a minute, I'll go inside and get a photograph."

The white-haired man disappeared and returned a few minutes later with an old picture. "I collect stuff on Oreville's past," he explained. "It's a hobby of mine."

Frank's eyes grew wide as he studied the photo. Grizzly Bear Lodge looked exactly like Mountain Hotel!

12   Ghosts

"Now we're getting somewhere!" Joe exclaimed, looking at the old photo. "You say this place burned down about fifty years ago? There's a hotel just a few miles out of town that looks just like it."

"Oh, you mean Mountain Hotel, where them movie folks are?" the old Oreville resident said. "That place wasn't built no more than ten years back. But you're right, it does look a whole lot like Grizzly Bear Lodge." Scratching his head, he took the photograph from Joe and studied it for a minute. Grizzly Bear Lodge and Mountain Hotel were almost identical, giving the impression that Mountain Hotel had been constructed as a replica of the old place.

After staring at the photograph another moment, the white-haired man handed it back to the boys. "Well!" he said with some surprise. "I knew the two places were similar, but I didn't realize they were that much alike. What are you kids up to, anyway?"

"We're just curious," Frank said casually. "Do you know why Grizzly Bear Lodge burned down? Was it an accident?"

The man shook his head. "It wasn't no accident. But they never found out who did it. You see, there was fighting going on in Oreville back then."

"Between the northsiders and the southsiders," Joe put in, remembering what Tim's father had told them about the origins of the feud.

"Right." Their host nodded slowly. "I spent a couple of years in the mines myself before they were shut down. So I guess you could call me a southsider. Anyhow," he went on, leaning against the front porch, "after one of the mine shafts caved in one day, things got pretty nasty between the two sides. About a week later, the Grizzly Bear Lodge burned to the ground. It was owned by the northsiders, and everybody was sure that the miners did it. That was the beginning of the feud."

"Tell us more about that cave-in," Joe asked, his breath visible in the cold air.

The Oreville resident laughed. "Let's go inside first before we freeze to death. I'll make some hot tea and tell you all I know."

Once inside the house, which was a small one-story structure just off Oreville's main street, their host motioned for the boys to sit at the kitchen table.

"I knew a few of the men who were killed in the cave-in," he said. "They were the more outspoken of the workers, trying to rally support for higher pay and better working conditions. That's why, when the shaft caved in, the other miners accused the owners of the company of purposely causing the accident—just to quiet the complainers down, if you know what I mean."

"What made the mine collapse?" Joe asked.

"A dynamite explosion," the old man replied.

Frank stroked his chin. "So the miners, or southsiders, believed that the owners deliberately set up the explosion to silence certain people?" he asked.

"I thought so myself," the old man admitted. "And I still wonder about it. Anyway, that's how the feud began. And that's why Grizzly

Bear Lodge was burned, along with other buildings."

"Do you know whether the place was looted before it was burned?" Joe queried, wondering if the Grizzly Bear Lodge stationery had been stolen at the time of the arson.

"No idea," the white-haired man replied. "Could've been, I guess."

The brothers thanked the old man for his help and told him they might be back for more information later on.

"Drop by any time." He smiled as he stood up from the table and saw them to the door. "I love to talk about the old days."

Once outside, Frank and Joe headed for the general store, a few blocks down the street. The local police car was parked outside.

"I'm beginning to see what Richard Chase was on to," Joe said excitedly. Then he stopped short and snapped his fingers. "We should go back and ask that old man about the chair lift operator, Ray Hodges. Maybe they know each other."

"You're right," Frank agreed. "But first I want to see what's happening with the townies."

At the general store, the boys found the police sergeant talking to several of the

110

Oreville boys, including Bob. The townies believed that Tim's friends were responsible for the attempted sabotage and named Rick and Paul as suspects.

The Hardys felt they could not voice their suspicions at this point, since it would only alert the movie company and foil Chet's chances to gather any proof.

Instead, Frank took Bob aside and out of the sergeant's earshot. "Will you be here in twenty minutes?" he asked.

"Yes."

"Good. I'd like you to get as many of your friends together and meet us here once the sergeant is gone."

Bob started to ask a question, but Frank had already turned to Joe and both left the store. They went to the old man's house.

"Back so soon?" he asked, chuckling.

"We have one last question," Joe said. "Do you know a man named Ray Hodges? He operates the main chair lift at the ski slopes."

"Sure I do. Ray has lived here his whole life, just like me. But he's a bit of a hermit. I don't know him well."

"Was he involved in the mining disaster in any way?" Joe went on.

"As a matter of fact," the old man replied,

"Ray's father was one of the people killed. He was probably the most ornery of all the miners and had made himself a kind of self-proclaimed leader for their cause."

"And does Ray have any brothers or cousins who look like him?" Frank asked.

"It seems he did," the old man said, focusing on the sky as he tried to remember. "He had a brother. Think his name was Larry or something. In fact, I remember that Ray and Larry were among the worst of the feuders back in the early days. They were only youngsters, but they were out there toting guns and marching in the streets just like the men. A couple of mean ones, they were."

"And where is Ray's brother now?" Frank went on.

The man threw up his hands. "I have no idea. Larry disappeared years ago. And Ray, as I said, doesn't socialize much anymore."

"Thanks very much," Frank beamed, shaking the man's hand. "You've been a great help."

Leaving the old miner standing on his front porch with a puzzled expression, the Hardys turned and walked down the steps.

"Wait a minute!" he called after them. "Do you know that movie actor, Richard Chase?"

Frank and Joe stared at him.

"No. Why do you ask?" Frank said, his face transformed with curiosity.

"'Cause he visited me about a week ago, and was asking the same sort of questions!"

"He was?" Joe looked baffled.

"Yep. He sure was. And now he's missing. You boys better be careful, whoever you are!" the old man warned.

The Hardys nodded silently and left. On the way to the general store, Frank said, "I bet Richard Chase realized that Larry Hodges is Ian Rider, the movie producer."

"And Rider found out that Chase knew, and it bothered him, so he moved Chase out of the way!" Joe added grimly.

"We'd better call Dad tonight," Frank said. "He can check out Hodges-Rider."

"For some reason," Joe said, "Rider built Mountain Hotel as a reproduction of Grizzly Bear Lodge. And he came across some of the original stationery, which he's now using as a prop in the movie. But I'm sure he's not calling the Horror Hotel Grizzly Bear Lodge just because there was some old stationery around."

"Maybe the Hodges brothers burned down the lodge after stealing the stationery and perhaps other things," Frank ventured. "And now, after making lots of money, Larry built his

113

own lodge just like the old one. It's as if he were sticking out his tongue at the wealthy mine owners and saying 'See, now it's mine!'"

"It sounds a little strange," Joe said. "But then, it appears as if the Hodges brothers and their father were all a little strange."

"What I can't figure out," Frank said, "is why Larry named the place Mountain Hotel except in the movie. And why did he change his name to Ian Rider?"

"Beats me," Joe said.

When they arrived at the general store, the police car was gone. Inside, Bob had gathered his friends together, and all were wondering what the Hardys were up to.

"We'd like you to take us to the mine shaft," Frank announced. "You guys know the mines inside out, and we want to do some exploring."

A hush fell over the room at Frank's request. The Oreville boys looked nervously at one another, apparently uneasy over Frank's suggestion.

"You're not setting us up for an ambush, are you?" Bob asked. "We're a little worried at this point about whose side you're on."

"If we were on the other guys' side, and knew they had turned on the gas, would we have prevented the explosion?" Frank asked, looking Bob straight in the eye.

"We only want to search for clues," Joe added. "The guy who played the monster disappeared into the mines and we want to check the place out."

But the boys were still apprehensive about going there, and Frank and Joe had the impression that it was not only an ambush they were concerned about. They seemed afraid of something else.

"We haven't been in the mines for years," Jay spoke up. "We really wouldn't be much help."

"That's right, we wouldn't know our way around anymore," Bret added.

Joe looked at the worried faces in the room. "What are you guys scared of?" he challenged the group.

"Ghosts!" a small voice uttered from a corner. "The mines are haunted!"

13   Trapped!

Frank and Joe turned toward the girl who had spoken. It was Lise, the petite brunette who had been at the store on the Hardys' first visit.

"Ghosts?" Joe queried. "What do you mean?"

Lise, who had been leaning against one of the video machines in the corner, fidgeted with her hands and looked at her friends. "I never heard it myself," she said. "But some people swear that they've heard the sound of dead miners at work in the shaft!"

"Let me explain," Bob took over. "We all used to play in the mines when we were kids. The headquarters of our club was in one of them. Then, about a year ago, a few of us were out there and we heard miners at work. We searched for the source of the sound and traced it to an old shaft which had caved in a long time ago and had buried some of our own grand-fathers alive."

"Are you talking about the disaster that hap-pened fifty years ago?" Frank asked. "The one that started the feud?"

Bob looked surprised. "You heard about that?"

Frank nodded. "Does it have something to do with your belief that the mines are haunted?"

"We didn't know what else to believe," Jay said. "Some of our relatives were killed in that cave-in, and when we heard miners from deep within that shaft, we figured it had to be their ghosts."

"Suppose it was real live people doing some mining," Joe suggested, trying to find a logical explanation for the sound.

"It couldn't be," Ben cried out, standing up from his chair and pacing around the room. "The shaft is totally buried, and there's no way to get in. The bodies weren't even recovered at the time!"

"They *had* to be ghosts!" Lise insisted.

"They were," Willie added. "I heard it myself, clear as day—the sound of picks and shovels from way inside the shaft!"

Although the sleuths found it hard to believe that there really were ghosts in the mines, they were more impressed by this ghost story than by others they had heard. The sound of miners at work, deep within a long buried shaft, could make anyone wonder. And since the bodies were never recovered, Frank and Joe understood the townies' fear of returning to the scene.

"You only heard the sound once?" Joe inquired.

"We went back a number of times," Ben replied. "Sometimes we heard it; sometimes we didn't."

"We haven't been there in almost a year," Willie admitted. "The place gives us the creeps now."

"Do you think you could come with us one more time?" Frank asked. "I'd like to check this thing out myself."

Not wanting to appear to be cowards, the boys, one by one, reluctantly agreed to accompany the young detectives to the mines.

"All right," Bob said. "But don't expect us to stay if the ghosts are at work again."

Frank nodded and led the group outside. They climbed into several cars, drove to the ski area, and parked. From there, they began to march through the woods to the far side of the mountain.

When they came to the entrance that was only partially boarded up, Bob and the others switched on the flashlights they had brought and went inside.

"This way," Bob said and turned left into a side shaft. The Hardys were right behind him and followed him through a maze of tunnels before coming to a halt. Bob shone his flashlight on a pile of rubble in front of them.

"This is the buried shaft?" Frank asked, gazing upon a heap of stones and boards that completely blocked the entrance to an adjoining mine.

"This is it," Bob confirmed. He trained his light on the rocks to show that there was no way to go any further.

"Are you sure?" Joe pressed.

"Yes. The explosion that caused the cave-in knocked out about fifty feet of the shaft," Bob replied. "The workers had no chance of getting out."

"Fifty feet!" Joe exclaimed. "How could you possibly hear ghosts behind fifty feet of rock?"

"It's very faint," Willie said. "We had to be quiet to hear it. It helps if you put your ear to the wall."

Frank and Joe leaned against the cold rock and pressed their ears against the wall.

Suddenly, Frank gasped. "I hear it!" he cried out.

From deep within the mine came the steady click of metal against stone. The townies quickly drew away. Fear showed in their faces, and for a moment no one spoke.

"Is that what you heard before?" Joe finally spoke up.

The boys nodded. They were clearly anxious to get out of the mine as soon as possible. Frank turned to Bob, who tried to remain calm.

"You say that the workers' bodies were never recovered?"

Bob cleared his throat before answering.

"That's right," he said. "Nobody really seems to know why. All I've heard is that an attempt was made, but they couldn't possibly get in there in time to find anyone alive. And then the feud got so bloody that everyone was too busy fighting."

"So all these people suffocated to death?" Joe asked.

Bob nodded. "I asked my parents many

times, but they don't want to talk about it. Neither does anyone else."

"Maybe some of the miners could have been rescued if people had tried hard enough," Ben added. "That's why I think their ghosts are haunting us now."

"Let's get out of here!" Willie urged. "And I don't ever want to come back."

Once more Frank and Joe put their ears to the wall. Again they heard the faint sound of a pick deep within the shaft. Both boys shuddered, thinking about the miners who had died underground so many years ago.

Then Joe pulled himself together. "There has to be an explanation for this!" he declared. "And it isn't ghosts. I don't—"

KER-BLAMMMMMM!

Suddenly an explosion ripped through the shaft.

"What was that?" Bob cried, his face ashen.

"I don't know, but I'm getting out of here," Willie gasped and ran away from the rock pile as fast as he could. Panic-stricken, the other boys followed, with Frank and Joe bringing up the rear. They hurried through the maze of shafts until they found themselves choking on the smoke and dust which swirled and spewed out all around them.

"Someone blew out the entrance!" Bob shouted.

A sinking feeling welled up in Joe's stomach as he stared at what had been the opening of the mine shaft. Now it was just a pile of dust and rocks, and not a single ray of light could be seen!

"We're trapped!" Ben cried amidst the confusion. "What are we going to do?"

Stricken with fear, the townies yelled for help. Frank and Joe began to cough from the swirling dust and pressed handkerchiefs to their mouths. "Just stay quiet!" Frank shouted. But no one paid attention.

"We shouldn't have come back!" one of the boys wailed. "I knew it. Now we're buried alive, too!"

Finally Frank managed to get himself heard. The dust settled down a bit, and the panic subsided. "You know these mines well," Frank said. "Is there another entrance?"

"There is!" Bob shouted, slapping his forehead with his palm. "How could we forget? We used to call it our secret entrance."

A groan went up from the crowd. "Boy, are we stupid!" Ben said. "But I suppose we got so excited and scared that we just didn't think of it."

"That's understandable," Frank said. "Why did you call it the secret entrance, though?"

"We found it when we were kids," Bob answered with a grin. "It's on the other side of the mines. Come on, let's go there."

Following a complex route, the boys made their way toward the secret mine entrance. On the way, angry talk was already flying back and forth on how to get back at Tim's group, whom everyone believed responsible for the explosion.

Frank and Joe tried to remind the townies that others may have been behind it, but no one listened. The boys were much too excited and angry.

"Here we are," Bob announced as they arrived at a small opening, big enough for only one person at a time.

One by one, they squeezed though, breathing deeply once they were out in the brisk winter air again. It took a while before their eyes adjusted to the bright light that reflected off the snow. The sky was clear and blue, and the midday sun poured through the trees.

"Boy, am I glad to be out of there," Willie said with a sigh, and dusted himself off. "We could have been killed!"

"Well, Lise knew we were going to the

mines," Joe reminded him. "If we hadn't come back, she would have organized a rescue squad."

Frank was looking over the area around the exit, some of which was protected by a rock outcropping and trees.

"Hey!" he exclaimed suddenly. "Look at this!"

Stooping down, the boys studied what appeared to be footprints. "These are the monster's tracks!" Joe cried out.

14 The Rescue Tunnel

Just visible in the snow under the overhang were the same gorilla tracks Frank and Joe had followed to the mines after Tim's accident. The prints let out of the secret entrance and down the hill.

"Those were made by that monster?" Bob asked.

"Yes," Frank replied. "Whoever wore that costume not only knew about the mines, but also about your secret entrance."

"Now we know why he didn't come out again," Frank said. "We waited for quite a while at the boarded-up shaft, but he never showed up."

"Now we're not saying you guys had something to do with it," Joe said. "But it sure looks strange, since supposedly you were the only ones who knew about the secret entrance."

"I told you we didn't steal that costume!" Bob cried defensively. "And we didn't cause Tim Adams's fall. But I can't explain how someone else knew about that entrance. I just don't know."

"Some of the old miners probably knew," Bret put in. "But I'm sure they'd have no reason to play monster."

Bob and Bret seemed sincere, but the Hardys felt that perhaps one of the group was working alone, or had conspired with the film company. They glanced from face to face, studying the various expressions. They also wondered if there might be a third entrance to the mines, one the townies didn't know about: one that might explain the noises deep within the caved-in shaft.

"I want to follow these tracks," Frank decided. "Are any of you interested in coming along?"

Of the eight Oreville boys, three agreed to join the Hardys. Bob was among them. The others wanted to go back to the mine's main entrance and look for signs of whoever had caused the explosion.

"Okay," Joe told them. "But be careful. There might be footprints in the snow, so don't walk around and destroy them."

The groups separated, and Frank led the way following the monster prints through the woods.

"The monster must've stayed in the mine a long time," Frank said. "When he finally came out of the secret entrance, it probably had stopped snowing."

The boys moved on, with Frank and Joe now falling behind the others. Frank nudged his brother. "Do you think Tim's friends blew up the mine entrance?" he asked.

"I don't know." Joe shrugged. "But I don't really think so. They didn't know we were out here, for one thing, and for another, I can't believe they'd do something like that."

"I agree," Frank replied. "I have a feeling that both groups are being framed."

"But why?" Joe wondered. "Now that the movie people filmed the accident, what could their motive be for all this other stuff?"

Frank frowned. "It seems that someone wants to escalate this feud, and is really trying to get the kids fighting seriously. Not just iceball battles, as before, but battles that can hurt and kill."

Joe slapped his right hand into the palm of his left. "I wish we could stop it before someone gets into real trouble!"

Frank nodded. "The monster guy knew the secret entrance to the mines," he said thoughtfully. "So he could have blown up the front of the shaft, figuring the townies could still escape. But it would have made them believe that Tim's friends had planned to trap them for good, and it would therefore make them more vicious than ever."

"But how did the culprit know the townies were in the mines?" Joe argued.

"Maybe he has a spy in the village," Frank reasoned.

"Hmm." Joe frowned. "This could also have another effect," he said. "Now the townies might believe we led them to the mines on purpose."

"I don't know about that," Frank said doubtfully. "We *were* trapped along with them!"

The brothers continued on foot through the woods, staying a short distance behind Bob and his friends. The monster tracks headed straight down the mountain, until they stopped at the edge of a road.

"Where does this go?" Frank asked as they caught up with the Oreville boys.

"It's just another access road to the ski area," Bob replied. "Looks like our friend the monster was picked up here, whoever he was."

"Let's check up and down the road a little way—maybe he entered the woods on the other side of the road," Frank suggested.

"Good idea," Bob shouted, and the boys split up. But after a few minutes they found nothing and returned to where the trail ended.

Disappointed that the tracks hadn't gone somewhere more exciting, like a cabin in the woods, the group of youths turned around and headed back toward the mines to join up with the others. As they came closer, they heard shouts through the woods.

"Come on!" Bob cried, breaking into a run. "It sounds like a fight."

When they reached the clearing in front of the now destroyed mine opening, Frank and Joe found the townies in an all-out fistfight with Tim's friends! Bob and his two buddies leaped right into the battle, but the Hardys held back.

"Hey, whose side are you on?" Paul shouted

angrily at the young detectives as he blocked a left jab from Jay. "Get in here and help us!"

"We don't want to fight!" Joe yelled. "And you shouldn't be fighting, either."

"Ah, forget about those two," another of Tim's friends yelled in disgust. "They're chicken!"

Frank and Joe bit their lips, but refused to join in the melee. The battle was intense, with no lack of bloody lips and noses. Several boys wrestled in the snow; others stood and boxed with their fists. With Bob and his two friends now in the fray, the Oreville gang soon had the upper hand, and Tim's group finally had to call it quits.

"Thanks a lot!" Rick spat sarcastically at the Hardys as he and his buddies ran into the woods. "Wait till we tell Tim about this!"

With torn clothing and battered bodies, the defeated crew made a hasty retreat. They cursed the townies as they left, promising to retaliate as soon as they could. The triumphant Oreville boys just laughed and challenged them to try it.

"Well!" Bob smiled at Frank and Joe as he dusted himself off. "I thought for a while that you two had led us here as part of a plan with those rich kids. I'm glad to see they're not your friends after all."

"Those rich kids, as you call them, *are* our friends," Frank said seriously. "But this isn't our fight."

"They *were* our friends," Joe said glumly. "Now I'm afraid we've made permanent enemies of them."

"I don't know how you can call those guys friends after they just about permanently buried you in the mines!" another boy said hotly.

"We're not at all sure they were responsible for it," Frank countered.

"Come off it!" Bob exclaimed. "How much evidence do you need? The mine was blown up, and then we caught Tim's friends red-handed, right outside the entrance!"

Frank and Joe realized that they would get nowhere in stopping the feud until they could prove who was behind the frame-up and why.

Discouraged, they parted from the Oreville boys and started around the mountain. "This isn't going very well," Joe muttered. "Tim's gang and the townies are both too caught up in their war to listen. On top of that, the movie people are on to us. And we have all these ideas of what may be behind it all, but we're no closer to proving it than we ever were. And Richard Chase is still missing."

"Something'll break soon!" Frank grinned assuringly. "I can feel it. We'll talk to Dad tonight. Maybe he's come up with something on that truck and the warehouse."

Joe did not reply. Silently, the brothers trudged back to the ski area, got their Ford from the parking lot, and drove to the Adams chalet.

"I hope we get to Tim before his friends do," Frank muttered as they entered the house.

Tim, who was still in bed, listened quietly to their story. "I'll see what I can do," he said with a frown. "But I doubt my friends will pay much attention at this point."

"I think we should report the explosion to the police," Frank said.

"Oh, that's all we need!" Tim protested. "The sergeant was here this morning and asked me about the sabotage attempt on the townies' headquarters. I told him we had nothing to do with it, but he gave me a stiff warning and told me he'd have all of us in jail if the fighting didn't stop immediately. You tell him about what happened at the mines, and he'll cart us *and* the townies off and lock us all up."

"Maybe that wouldn't be such a bad idea," Joe said. "Then you couldn't fight anymore."

"Why don't you get out of here and leave me alone!" Tim was angry.

"All right, don't fly off the handle," Joe said. "We're not telling the police. But I just hope someone doesn't get seriously hurt before we find the real culprit behind all this."

Feeling frustrated, the Hardys left Tim's room and settled down on the living room sofa. They were hoping Chet would be back from Mountain Hotel soon with new leads in the case.

"I bet Richard Chase found out something that had to do with that old mining disaster," Frank said. "I'd like to study up on that some more."

"I wonder if the old man we talked to this morning would know if there are any records," Joe said.

"Let's ask him," Frank suggested. "But first I'd like to call Dad."

To their relief, they found their father in his hotel room. "Good news!" Mr. Hardy said excitedly over the receiver. "I found out that the film director changed his name to Ian Rider ten years ago. It used to be Larry Hodges."

"We figured that," Joe said. "Did you learn anything else? Like what that truck was unloading?"

"I'm working on that," his father told him. "Let me get back to you later."

After Joe had informed Mr. Hardy of what had happened in Oreville, he hung up. "Let's go talk to the old man again," he said.

The young detectives found the local historian at his house. He showed them blueprints of the mine shafts, which he had salvaged from the mining company records.

"We were told that the miners' bodies were never recovered," Frank said, putting down the blueprints for a minute. "We also heard something about their ghosts still haunting the mines."

"Oh, yes!" the old-timer said with a twinkle in his eye. "The ghosts of those fellows are still in there. Sometimes they come into town, late at night when the wind blows out of the north. They remind us how they were never dug out. They were buried alive, and they ain't never going to forgive us. Not ever."

"But why was the rescue attempt not carried through?" Joe asked.

"Well, we tried," their host said. "We dug a tunnel straight down from the top of the mountain, since it was the shortest distance to the end of the shaft. But it took so long that no one had any hopes of finding anybody alive.

Then the feud got so heavy that it was like a regular war and everybody was needed to defend themselves and their families."

"Where is the tunnel?" Frank inquired eagerly.

The old man took the blueprints. "Right about here," he said, pointing to a spot on the mountain. "Where the slopes are now. The original shaft went so far through the mountain that it almost reached the other side. The end of it ain't more than twenty or thirty feet from the surface at one point. That's why it was a lot easier to dig a new tunnel there than to evacuate the exploded part."

"And yet it was never finished," Frank said. "I can't understand that."

"Well, the work was hard. Back then we didn't have the modern drilling equipment they got these days. So people gave up hope after a while. They would have continued in order to retrieve the bodies, but the fighting, as I told you before, got out of hand. Some of the men were killed and everybody was more concerned with protecting themselves rather than digging up corpses."

"But what about later?" Joe questioned. "Why didn't they resume the work?"

The old man shrugged. "I don't really know.

I've always had an uneasy feeling about that. So did a lot of other people. And I tell you, those fellows are still working down there—at least their ghosts are!"

"What kind of mine was it?" Frank asked.

"Copper," the man replied. "We mined copper and some zinc."

The boys thanked their host and left his house. As they were walking down the front steps, the late afternoon sun was starting to sink below the crest of the mountain, and a bone-chilling wind blew steadily through the small town.

"Joe," Frank said and took his brother's arm. "I have a feeling that the unfinished tunnel has something to do with those ghostly sounds we heard. If I only knew what!"

15 A Confrontation

"We have to watch that lift operator, Ray Hodges," Joe said, zipping up his parka as they headed for their car. "Whatever is going on, I bet he's in on it. Otherwise he would have told us that his brother is the producer of the movie."

"And Rider wouldn't have denied having any relatives in the area," Frank added. "It's obvious the Hodges brothers are hiding something. But I don't think it would be to our advantage to confront either of them at this point. We'll have to do a little more investigating first."

"Like taking a look at that tunnel," Joe agreed. "Maybe we'll find it if we go over the top of the mountain carefully."

Since it was growing dark, the boys postponed their search until the next day. They drove to the Adams chalet, hoping to get an update from Chet or their father.

Chet was reading when the Hardys walked into the house. "Here," he said, pointing to the pages he had already finished. "I got a copy of the revised film script. The director just finished making all the changes and handed copies around to everyone."

"Terrific," Frank said, and both he and Joe began poring over the material. Tim's accident was now in the script, and so were several other new scenes.

"I saw the rushes today, too," Chet announced. "You were right. It seemed as if the monster scene was planned. The camera angle was just right. They knew it was going to happen!"

"That's what we figured," Joe said. "Did you see any of the later scenes, too?"

Chet nodded.

"How did *you* look?" Frank asked.

Chet shrugged. "Fat. They made a fool of me. All you see is me huffing and puffing with that creepy creature after me. They even made a close-up of my tummy bouncing up and down. Of course, everyone was laughing when they saw it. I was so embarrassed."

Frank and Joe could barely keep from laughing themselves as they thought of Chet's remarkable belly filling the movie screen.

"Well, that's the price of stardom," Joe joked. "Why don't you go on a diet?"

"And lose the only thing that got me the part?" Chet challenged. "What's a little embarrassment compared with being in the movies?"

"Does the director need you for any more scenes?" Frank inquired.

"Not really," Chet replied. "Tomorrow they'll be filming on the slopes again. They want extras for a crowd scene, though. I thought I'd volunteer."

Chet flipped to a page toward the end of the script. "The director says he's going to reshoot the hotdogging competition. He wants to get some crowd reaction and some close-ups of Tim."

"He must be kidding!" Frank protested. "Tim's got a concussion and a sprained ankle! He can't—"

"Yes, I can!" came Tim's voice from the doorway as he hobbled into the room. "It cost me enough to get this part. I don't want to blow it now!"

"Even after knowing the film company

caused your accident in the first place?" Joe asked in disbelief. "If I were you, I wouldn't go near those guys."

"And are you well enough to get back on skis?" Frank put in. "The doctors said to take it easy for a while. It's only been—"

The young skier laughed. "I talked to the director this morning. He said all I had to do was stand there for the close-ups. I won't have to ski. And I don't think he'll try anything like that monster stunt again, so I may as well get my beautiful face in the movies while I have the chance."

Frank and Joe had to laugh. Then they turned to the script again. The story specified that after Tim took his fall, the monster was to be chased from the slope by a Sno-cat, a bulldozerlike machine used to groom the slopes. Finally the hairy creature was to be crushed to death.

"Did you find out who's playing the monster?" Joe asked Chet.

"Another actor like me," the boy replied. "I met him after the shooting. He seemed to be on the level."

Frank now turned to Tim. "Tell me something," he said. "What were your friends doing at the mines today? Did they say?"

"Oh Ricky and Paul? They came over today

and followed the townies' tracks, out of curiosity," Tim replied. "But they didn't blow up the entrance, if that's what you're getting at."

Frank nodded. "I'm inclined to believe you," he said. "But then, who did it?"

"Did you find any other clues today?" Joe asked Chet when no one had an answer to Frank's question.

"Nothing," Chet replied. "I tried to keep an eye on those equipment trucks, but I didn't notice anything out of the ordinary."

"By the way," Tim said, "My friends Ricky and Paul aren't too happy with you fellows. You ought to stay away from them until they cool off."

"Okay, thanks," Joe said.

Just then the phone rang. Tim picked it up, then handed it to Frank. "It's your father," he said.

Mr. Hardy had uncovered some new evidence. "I traced the horror movie's shady financial backers to a gang which is known to deal in the illegal sale of precious metals," he reported. "The men with the knives that you tangled with twice are connected to that gang."

"That's interesting," Frank said. "Did you find out what was in those crates? They seemed awfully heavy, and speaking about metals—"

"I'm working on that," Mr. Hardy answered. "I'll call you as soon as I come up with something."

Frank hung up. The mention of precious metals again brought the "ghost miners" to mind, and he was now more eager than ever to locate the unfinished rescue tunnel to the buried shaft.

"Thanks," Joe said, then yawned. It was getting late and the young detectives were tired.

"Let's go to bed," Frank said. "We need to be alert tomorrow for our search of the tunnel."

In the morning, the boys and Mr. Adams drove to the ski area. On the way, they filled him in on what had happened the previous day.

"Do you know about that unfinished rescue shaft?" Frank inquired.

Mr. Adams shrugged. "I've heard about it. But I don't know where it is. As I told you, I was too young at the time to really remember. But what worries me is the Hodges brothers. They used to be real troublemakers."

"I bet," Frank said.

"Let me ask if any of the people around here know Ray well," Mr. Adams went on. "Perhaps I can pick up some clues."

"Thanks," Joe said as they all got out of the parking lot. "We'll check with you later."

Before putting on their skis, the Hardys picked up a trail map of the ski area and compared it to what they remembered of the blueprint that the old man in town showed them.

"Just as we thought!" Frank exclaimed. "It must be right near Hodges's booth at the top of the main lift!"

A few minutes later, the young detectives boarded the chair lift. On their way up, they could see the film company setting up on the slopes. Chet and Tim were among the people assembled for the day's shooting. Dutton Foster was organizing the scene, re-creating the appearance of the freestyle competition.

At the top of the lift, Hodges's sleepy-eyed face again appeared at the window of the booth. This time, he seemed to show some interest in the Hardys.

"Shall we talk to him?" Joe asked.

"We might as well," Frank said. "He knows who we are. If we confront him, maybe he'll say something that'll give us a clue."

Upon dismounting, the young detectives went directly to the booth and opened the door.

"What do you want this time?" Ray glared at them.

"We want to know why you lied to us," Frank said evenly. "We know about your brother,

Larry. He's the owner of Mountain Hotel and the producer of the movie."

"So what? It's none of your business!" came the curt reply.

"Richard Chase is our business," Joe spoke up, studying Hodges's face for his reaction to the name.

Hodges was speechless. He looked like a cornered animal, and a few seconds passed before he composed himself. "What makes you think I know anything about Chase?" he finally asked in a subdued voice.

"We have our reasons," the blond boy replied. "And if you want to keep the police out of this, you can show us the tunnel."

"Tunnel? What tunnel?" Hodges gulped, his eyes widening.

"The tunnel to the buried mine shaft!" Frank said.

Hodges froze for a moment, then stepped backward, grabbed a shovel from the wall of the booth, and raised it menacingly!

16 Chet in Danger

"Don't try anything foolish!" Joe warned, raising one of his ski poles and pointing it at the man.

After looking at the sharp end of the ski pole, Hodges dropped the shovel. Then a smile crossed his face. "You kids have been lucky so far," he said. "But don't push it or you'll find yourselves in over your heads. Understand?"

"Fine," Frank said. "We'll just have to locate that tunnel ourselves."

The boys closed the booth door and skied away. Then they scouted the area, hoping the tunnel opening would be in sight. However, after a thorough search, they had found nothing.

Frank was disappointed. "I thought that tunnel had something to do with those noises we heard in the mines," he said. "Now I wonder. Maybe it was filled in years ago and doesn't even exist anymore. There certainly isn't any sign of it in this area!"

Discouraged, the boys skied down the mountain until they came to the point where the movie company was filming.

Both Tim's friends and some of the townies were among the extras for the crowd scene. While tensions were high between the two groups, they managed to restrain themselves from fighting.

Frank gazed up the slope. The Sno-cat, manned by a man wearing a ski mask, was plowing down the hill in pursuit of the monster. Cameramen were stationed above and below the action, and the bearded director shouted orders to the extras.

"Make it look good!" he yelled. "You're scared. Real scared! Show it!"

The crowd pretended to disperse in panic as the Sno-cat bore down in pursuit of the horrible creature.

"There's Chet," Frank said, picking their friend out among the many people.

Chet screamed and waved his hands in the

air as he fled from monster and machine.

"What a ham," Joe laughed.

Suddenly, the Snow-cat made an abrupt turn in Chet's direction!

"Watch out!" Frank and Joe cried in unison.

Hearing the cry, Chet turned to find the steel treads of the massive vehicle heading right at him!

"YAAAAHHHHH!!!"

Panic-stricken, he dove out of the way of the Sno-cat, landing belly-first in the snow just a few feet from its path.

"Come on," Joe said angrily as he started toward their buddy. "Let's get him out of there."

The two youths skied over to Chet, who was wiping the snow off his face.

"Th ... th ... they tried to kill me!" Chet shuddered.

"We saw it." Frank tried to be calm. "It's not safe around here anymore, for any of us. Whatever's going on, it's no small operation. And now they're on to us for sure. They know we're hot on their trail and mean business. So don't expect any more scare tactics. From now on they'll be playing for real!"

Somberly, Frank, Joe, and Chet skied down to the lodge and took off their skis.

"I hope they don't try anything with Tim,"

Chet said, remembering that their friend was still on the slopes.

"You'd better warn him," Joe said. "But be careful. We'll be inside talking to his father."

Chet nodded, put his skis back on, and boarded the chair lift. Meanwhile, the Hardys went into the lodge to find Mr. Adams.

The resort owner waved to them from one of the lunch tables in the cafeteria. Sitting with him was an elderly man dressed in coat and tie. Mr. Adams introduced him as Mr. Sage, the manager of the cafeteria.

"Mr. Sage tells me he used to work in the mines," Tim's father said, getting to the point. "And he has an idea that you two might like to hear."

The cafeteria manager cleared his throat. "I don't know Ray too well," he apologized. "Nobody does. He lives by himself outside of town and doesn't like to keep much company."

"I talked to several employees," Mr. Adams confirmed. "Nobody seems to be at all close to him these days."

"But I used to know Ray's father, Bill Hodges, when Ray and Larry were teenagers," the old man went on. "We worked in the mine together.

"Bill Hodges was a loner himself until he

began to get involved in the dispute over conditions in the mines. Then he became a sort of leader, a champion of the miners' rights and all that. The funny thing, though, was that Bill was also acting like he was going to quit the mines soon. Right before he got buried in the cave-in, he got drunk one night at the bar and started bragging about how he was going to be rich. Nobody gave it much thought at the time, but we all knew he was acting strange."

"We heard that the mining disaster was caused by a dynamite explosion," Frank said.

"That's another funny thing." The old man nodded. "Bill was in charge of the dynamite and he knew how to use it. If it wasn't for the fact that he was killed in the explosion himself, some of us might've wondered about him. Instead, we all blamed it on the mine owners, since they were the ones with the motive for shutting us up."

"But you suspect Mr. Hodges caused the explosion himself?" Joe asked.

The ski area employee shifted in his chair. "Well, I know it sounds crazy, Bill being one of our leaders and himself being killed in the cave-in. I never said anything to anyone else, 'cause there was no proof and they would've just laughed at me, or worse. But he had been behaving in a strange way, and I always had this suspicion in the back of my head."

"But why would he want to blow up the mine shaft with himself and the others in it?" Joe queried.

"Maybe he didn't intend it that way," Frank answered for the old miner. "Maybe Bill Hodges had a plan and it backfired."

The cafeteria manager smiled, happy that the boys weren't taking him for a total fool. "That's what I wondered myself."

"And you never told anyone about this?" Joe asked.

"No," the man answered. "What good would it have done? Bill Hodges and the rest of those miners were local heroes. They're why the northsiders and southsiders went to war with each other. If I'd come out saying that one of our own leaders had caused the explosion, they would've strung me up right then and there!"

"Let's assume that Bill Hodges *was* the victim of his own scheme, whatever it was," Frank said. "What would his sons have to do with it?"

"I don't know," the man sighed. "I just thought you might be interested, since Mr. Adams said you were investigating Ray and the feud."

"We *are* interested. And thanks for your

help," Frank said warmly and stood up.

Before leaving, he and Joe got the address of Ray Hodges's home. They then walked out to the parking lot and climbed into their rented Ford.

"I think it's a farfetched idea," Joe remarked, taking the driver's seat.

"I would agree with you, except for one thing," Frank replied. "It seems that the rescue tunnel wasn't completed for a reason, as if someone wanted to prevent the miners from digging it."

"I don't get it," Joe said. "The old man told us the reason it wasn't finished was the fight!"

"Let's say Bill Hodges caused that explosion on purpose," Frank said, "perhaps to hide something he had found at the end of the mine shaft. And let's say, for some reason, his plan backfired and he ended up killing himself and some others. Naturally, the people would believe that the northsiders were responsible for the explosion, making Bill and the others out to be martyrs."

"Which got the feud going," Joe added.

"Right. Now, let's say that Bill Hodges's two sons, Ray and Larry, knew about their father's secret. Then, after the cave-in, they didn't want the rescuers digging the tunnel."

"Because they worried that people would find out about their father's scheme," Joe said.

"Right again. Now, what do Ray and Larry do? They escalate the feud and prevent the rescue attempt. They do everything in their power to keep everybody busy fighting."

"I see what you're getting at," Joe agreed. "To protect their father's reputation, they set fire to the Grizzly Bear Lodge, among other things, and ran through town toting guns."

Frank looked at his younger brother. "Perhaps they're still doing it," he said slowly. "Perhaps they're using the feud to this day to cover up some secret!"

"We must find that rescue tunnel," Joe declared. "I bet the key to the mystery is right there!"

"Yes. We'll have to make another search right around the chair lift operator's booth. But first, let's check out Ray Hodges's house for clues."

"Here it is," Joe announced, pulling into a driveway at the outskirts of town. He stopped next to a small, rundown bungalow set behind a cluster of pine trees. No other cars were in sight.

"Let's walk around and see if we come up with something," Frank said as they got out of the car. The boys split up, each checking one side of the house, peering into windows as they went. Soon Frank's voice came from the backyard.

"Hey," he called. "There's a tool shed here!"

Joe hurried to his brother and saw a small aluminum structure. The door was open, so the boys stuck their heads inside.

A collection of mining equipment lay on the floor—picks, shovels, miner's helmets, and other accessories. Although old, the tools had recently been used. None were rusted, and the tips of the picks shone bright.

"That clinches it!" Frank cried. "It accounts for the so-called ghost miners!"

"And look over there," Joe pointed.

Frank gasped. "Wooden crates, just like the ones the truck driver delivered to the warehouse!"

Joe inspected the boxes. "Except these are empty!" he declared.

17   Standoff at Windy Rock

"This is the proof we need!" Joe said excitedly. "Let's tell Tim and his friends before they and the townies start any more trouble!"

The young detectives drove back to the ski area, hoping to meet the boys on the slopes. But when they arrived, none of them were there, not even Chet.

The Hardys drove to the Adams chalet, found it empty, and continued on to the general store. But even there they had no luck.

"Maybe trouble has started already!" Joe said anxiously as they were leaving the store. Just then Ben came into view walking down the main street. The Hardys got into their car and drove up to him.

"What's going on?" Joe inquired. "Where is everybody?"

"At Windy Rock!" Ben said, sounding upset. "They have baseball bats and switchblades, and I'm worried. You have to stop them!"

"They what!" Frank exclaimed.

"Bob, Jay, Rick, Paul, all of them!" Ben cried. "They drove out there for a big fight. Some of the kids took weapons. I was too scared to go. I think somebody's going to get killed!"

"Where's Windy Rock?" Frank asked.

"I'll lead you there," Ben replied and stepped into the car. "Do you think you can stop them?"

"We'll try," Joe told the frightened youth.

Following Ben's directions, the Hardys took the road north. The sunlight was fading fast behind the mountains and night would soon be upon them.

"How long ago did they leave?" Frank asked.

"About an hour. Just after filming was over on the ski slopes. They were really mad at each other."

"Any new reason?" Joe queried.

"The movie crew staged a fight scene," Ben explained. "The whole thing was supposed to be faked, but some of the guys really started hitting each other."

"Sounds like another one of the director's

bright ideas," Joe said to his brother.

"Anyway," the Oreville youth went on, "when it was all over everyone decided to go up to Windy Rock and have it out."

"Did a fat boy go with them?" Fran asked, wondering about Chet.

"Not that I remember," Ben said. "I don't know for sure, though. Make a left here."

Joe turned the Ford onto a steep and narrow road which took them up the side of a nearby mountain. Windy Rock, Ben told them, was a lookout point at the road's highest elevation. As they went up, they could see the surrounding countryside drop away behind them. The town of Oreville was visible in the valley below, and there was a clear view of the ski area.

By the time the Ford arrived at Windy Rock, the sun had sunk beneath the mountains.

"There are the cars," Joe said, nodding toward a line of vehicles parked just off the road.

"I hope we're not too late," Frank put in grimly.

Windy Rock was a large section of cliff which jutted out from the side of the mountain. It was devoid of trees. A few shrubs clung to the clumps of rocks, the only places offering shelter from the chilly winter wind.

"Boy, it's cold up here." Joe shivered as he

climbed from the car.

Zipping up their parkas, the three youths walked briskly out on the rock to find the others.

"There they are!" Ben shouted, spotting a dozen or more figures in an open area.

Two groups of boys stood facing each other, engaged in a shouting match. People made threatening gestures with baseball bats or knives, but it was clear that the fight hadn't actually started yet.

"I think both sides are in over their heads," Frank said. "They don't really want to fight, but they don't want to lose face, either."

Joe nodded. "It's a classic standoff."

Followed by Ben, the Hardys walked toward the boys. When Bob saw them coming, he yelled, "Stay out of this! This is none of your business!"

"Listen! This feud was set up!" Joe called back. "We can prove it. The film company wanted you fighting to cover up its activities. As a matter of fact, the producer started this whole thing many years ago. His name is really Larry Hodges and—"

"Stay out of this!" another voice interrupted. It was Tim. He stood with Rick and Paul, who had brought ski poles along as weapons.

"Why don't you just come back to town and listen!" Joe pleaded. "We can explain everything, and what's more, we can prove it!"

But instead of talking the hostile youths out of their battle, the Hardys' efforts seemed to have the opposite effect. Slowly, the two groups began to advance on each other, scared, but not wanting to appear cowardly.

"Hey!" one of the boys cried suddenly. "Something's on fire!" He pointed to a spot in the valley below.

In the distance, a building was ablaze. Bright flames leaped high into the sky, lighting up a billowing mass of smoke.

"It's at the ski area!" Tim shouted.

"We'd better check it out," Bret cried. Welcoming the excuse to call off the fight, the boys ran for their cars. Soon, a caravan of automobiles was on its way back down the winding road.

"That's what I call perfect timing," Joe uttered with relief as he drove the Ford toward town.

"Don't count your chickens too quickly," Frank warned. "Those guys will still come to blows sooner or later unless we can convince them not to."

Curious about the fire, the Hardys followed

the boys up the access road to the ski area. When they reached it, they saw fire trucks in the parking lot. The structure that was burning was an extension of the lodge containing a gift and ski apparel shop.

By the time the boys got out of their cars, the fire was almost extinguished. The Hardys and the others joined the crowd of onlookers.

Just then, the police sergeant stepped out from among the firemen and walked briskly toward the youths. "All right, I've had enough of this!" he shouted. "All you kids are under arrest!"

"For what?" Tim asked in disbelief.

"Arson!" the sergeant bellowed. "I've been talking to the fire chief, and he's convinced someone set this fire."

"But we weren't even here!" Bob protested. "We were all up at Windy Rock. You can—"

"I don't want to hear any more of your excuses," the sergeant cut him short. "I'm taking you down to the station and I'm not letting anyone go until I receive some straight answers. Get in your cars and follow me! All of you!"

"Now do you believe someone is purposely framing you?" Frank asked Bob as he and Joe accompanied the townie to his car.

"I'm ready to believe anything," Bob replied grimly.

The Hardys watched the line of vehicles trailing the sergeant out of the lot. "It's just as well they were arrested," Joe said. "Now they won't be able to get at each other for a while. We can go down and explain to Sergeant Baker that Ray and Larry Hodges are the guilty ones."

Frank nodded. "I'm glad we weren't arrested, too! But you know, I'm wondering what happened to Chet."

Chet Morton had not been at Windy Rock, nor at the fire. In fact, the Hardys realized they hadn't seen their chubby friend since his close call with the Sno-cat that afternoon.

"We'd better look for him," Joe said, and the two went back to the site of the fire. It was now a smoldering heap of burned wood, and the onlookers were dispersing. Chet was not among them.

"Hey!" Joe said, pointing to a group of medics who were surrounding a figure on a stretcher. "Someone must've been in the building when it caught fire."

Frank and Joe quickly walked over to the victim.

It appeared to be a man, but his face was unrecognizable because of the gauze pads the medics had applied to his forehead and cheeks.

Frank and Joe's hearts beat wildly as the same thought raced through their minds. Was the figure on the stretcher Chet Morton?

18 Arson

The Hardys' eyes traveled from the injured man's face to his body, and they sighed in relief. The burned victim was much too slender to be Chet!

"Was this man in the building when it burned?" Frank asked one of the medics.

"Yes," came the reply. "He'll be all right. Got some minor burns on his face and is suffering from smoke inhalation. We'll take him to the hospital, but he'll be out in a day or two. He was lucky."

"I don't feel so lucky!" the man on the stretcher groaned as he opened his eyes.

Frank kneeled down next to him. "Do you

have any idea who did this?" he asked. "Did you see anyone around?"

"No," the man replied weakly. "The fire started very fast. But I could smell gasoline, so I'm sure it was no accident."

"What were you doing in the shop?" Joe queried. "Wasn't it closed?"

The fire victim studied the Hardys with curiosity. "Who are you? Cops?"

"No, but we're detectives," Frank explained. "And we think this fire ties in with a case we're working on."

"Case?" the man asked. "You mean you know who burned the shop?"

"Possibly. We'll tell you about it later. Now we'd like to hear your story."

"Well," the man said, "I just moved up here a few weeks ago to run the shop. Since I didn't have a place to live yet, I set up a cot in the back room for the time being."

"And that's where you were when the fire broke out?" Frank asked.

"Yes. And now I don't have anywhere to stay!"

Frank thought of inviting the man to the Adams chalet, but decided he'd better ask Tim's father first. "We'll try to find you accommodations," he promised, then stood up. "Come on, Joe," he said. "Let's go back to the scene of the crime."

"Do you think it was another ploy to escalate the feud?" Joe asked as they looked over the burned building for clues.

"I suspect it's more than that," Frank replied. He stood where the ski shop had been and gazed around. "Anyone staying at the shop would have a clear view of the chair lift," he said.

"You mean, it was burned down because someone didn't want to be watched?"

"Could be. The sabotage attempt at the general store and the mine explosion could have been staged to lead up to this, so the blame would go to the kids in all cases."

"You mean the Hodges strategy? Escalate the feud to cover up for something?"

"Exactly. Show the people that the kids are capable of arson and setting explosives. Then no one would doubt that they burned the ski shop, too."

"But why would someone want to prevent the man in the ski shop from seeing the lift at night? It isn't even running after four."

Frank shrugged. "It's something we have yet to figure out. But first we have to find Chet!"

The boys hurried to their Ford and drove out of the parking lot. The stopped at the Adams chalet, but no one was home.

"Maybe Mr. Adams is down at the police station," Frank ventured.

"Chet could be with him," Joe said.

"I doubt it," Frank declared. "He wasn't near the fire scene. Let's check Mountain Hotel. He may have gone there."

A few minutes later, Frank and Joe pulled up in front of the film site. Cautiously, they approached the building and looked inside.

"Frank!" Joe gasped. "There's Chet in the lobby!"

Chet was, indeed, sitting among some of the actors, talking and apparently enjoying himself!

"Shall we go in?" Joe wanted to know.

"Let's wait out here for a moment," Frank advised. "I'd like to keep an eye on the place and see what happens."

The young detectives headed for a clump of bushes near the front porch. Suddenly, two figures jumped out from behind the shrubbery and lunged at them. They were the same two hoodlums the boys had tangled with before. Only this time they weren't carrying knives— they brandished tire irons instead!

"Finally we've got you!" one of the men

growled. He grabbed Joe by the arm and roughly shoved him toward the back of the hotel. The other thug did the same with Frank.

When they had reached the trucks that were parked in the rear, the boys were forced inside the nearest one.

"Give me your car keys!" one of their attackers demanded, holding his tire iron threateningly over the boys' heads.

Reluctantly, Joe complied. Then the man slammed the truck's back door shut and locked it. It was totally dark inside the cargo compartment, and the Hardys had to feel around to get their bearings.

"Seems that the only thing in here is a bunch of empty crates!" Frank declared.

"I wonder what they are planning to do with us," Joe moaned.

Just then the truck started up. The Hardys could feel it drive away from the hotel and turn onto the road. They sat on the crates and wondered where they were headed, what the crooks had in store for them, and how they could escape!

Ten minutes passed before the truck came to a stop. The young detectives heard the cab door open and close, then footsteps heading near the back. A moment later the latch was unhooked.

"All right, get out!" one of the thugs ordered the boys as he opened the door. "Come on, hurry—"

"*Ouuuwww!*" Suddenly both men bellowed as they were greeted by flying crates landing on their heads with enough force to knock them to the ground.

A second later, the Hardys were upon them, grabbing the tire irons from their hands and wrestling the thugs to the pavement.

"Okay, now it's your turn!" Joe commanded. "Into the truck!"

The boys shoved the dazed crooks into the cargo compartment, then locked the door.

"Good work!" Frank congratulated his brother as he dusted himself off.

"You weren't so bad yourself." Joe grinned. Then he looked around. They were in a remote section of the mountain road, which wound precariously along the edge of a steep cliff. There was no sign of any buildings or traffic in the area.

"I wonder why they brought us here," Joe said.

"Your guess is as good as—hey! There's our car!"

The Ford was parked a short distance from the truck. Evidently, one of the men had driven

169

it while the other had been behind the wheel of the truck.

Frank grabbed Joe's arm. "You know what their scheme was?" he said. "They were going to send us over the cliff in our car!"

Joe gulped, looking over the side to a rocky creek bed sixty feet below. "They probably planned to knock us out with the tire irons, stuff us in the car, and push it over. This way it would look like an accident."

"Phew!" Frank said. "That sure was a close call."

Luckily the keys to the Ford and the truck were both still in the ignitions. "I'll drive the truck back," Frank suggested. "You follow in the car."

"Are we taking these two thugs to the police?" Joe asked.

"Not just yet. I have a hunch I want to follow at the ski area first," Frank replied. "I also want to call Dad."

The young detectives drove to the Adams chalet to make the phone call.

"I've been trying to reach you all evening," Mr. Hardy said when he got on the line. "I found out what was in those crates."

"What?" Frank asked.

"Platinum!"

19 *Operation at Midnight*

"Platinum!" Frank repeated, excited. Then he gave his father a brief summary of the situation, promising to call him back as soon as possible.

"You mean the crates contained a precious metal?" Joe said when his brother had hung up.

"Yes, and it only confirms my hunch," Frank said. "Let's go. We have no time to spare."

"Where are we going?'

"To the ski area. And let's take the truck." He was already out the door.

"Hey, won't you let me in on whatever you're thinking?" Joe demanded.

"In the truck!"

Frank was already behind the wheel of the

truck and Joe slid in next to him. The two thugs were cursing and pounding on the sides, demanding to be set free immediately. Joe was bursting with curiosity, but the ruckus made any conversation between the brothers impossible.

A few minutes later, Frank swung the truck into the parking lot. The firefighters were gone, and the area was dark and deserted.

"This should do it," Frank said as he stopped near one end of the lodge, directly opposite the chair lift. "Now we wait."

A moment later, they heard the faint sound of an engine starting up.

"The lift!" Joe cried. "Look, it's running!"

Just visible in the dark, the chairs began moving.

"I was right!" Frank beamed. "Now let's go for a ride."

The young detectives leaped from the truck and ran to the boarding station. Soon they were moving up the mountain in one of the empty chairs.

"I think we caught the gang red-handed!" Frank said, staring ahead into the darkness. "It all fit together when Dad mentioned platinum."

"I've figured it out," Joe said. "The Hodges brothers are mining platinum from the buried shaft and removing it through the now finished rescue tunnel."

"Correct," Frank said. "Then they transport it down the chair lift and load it on the truck. That's why they had to get the man in the ski shop out of the way, so he wouldn't see them!"

"Then they take the stuff to the warehouse, where Rider-Hodges disposes of it."

"You've got it," Frank said.

"But was it a good idea to take the lift up?" Joe asked worriedly. "We're rolling right into their hands!"

"No, we're not," Frank said. "Remember, about thirty feet from the end station, there's a stretch where the lift is only about six feet off the ground. We get off there and walk the rest of the way, then sneak up to the top and watch!"

Joe grinned. "Good idea." Then he grabbed Frank's arm in a sudden motion. "Oh, no!" he gasped.

Out of the night, the figure of Ray Hodges appeared. He was riding the lift down the mountain! Several chairs in back of him were loaded with large bundles.

When he noticed the boys, the lift operator was momentarily startled. But as he passed by, he emitted an evil laugh!

"What do we do now?" Joe groaned, feeling

helpless. Suspended by the cable, the chairs hung high over the slopes, and there was no way for them to jump off!

"When he gets to the bottom, he'll probably turn off the lift," Frank said.

Sure enough, a few moments later the motor was shut off, leaving Frank and Joe dangling in the freezing night air. From their perch, they could see the lodge and the parking lot far below. They watched as Hodges opened the back of the truck and released his confederates. Then the three men started loading the bundles into the crates and stacking them in the back of the truck.

"We've got to get down!" Joe said, his teeth beginning to chatter from the cold. "They're going to escape!"

"Not without the truck keys, they won't," Frank said as he patted his pants pocket. "Not for a while anyway. But you're right, we have to get down. They'll be after us in a minute."

The boys surveyed the lift. They were close to one of the support poles, but in order to reach it, they would have to shimmy along the cable for a few feet. It would be an extremely dangerous undertaking.

"Look!" Frank said suddenly. "They're coming for us in the Sno-cat!"

They heard the sound of its engine starting up, and the huge machine began to move up the mountain.

"Okay. Let's go!" Joe said nervously. He pulled himself up the thin steel rod holding the chair. Then he grabbed the overhead cable. The metal was ice cold and his leather gloves offered little protection. But with enormous willpower, Joe managed to make his way hand-over-hand until he reached the support pole. Frank was close behind him, and when Joe saw that he was dangling forty feet above ground, a shiver went down his spine.

But he forced himself to think only of what lay ahead and started to climb down the ladder rungs on the pylon. A moment later Frank reached the pole, too.

"Wow!" Joe sighed when he finally jumped to the ground. "I almost lost my grip up there a couple of times."

"So did I," Frank admitted and stuck his freezing hands inside his pockets for warmth. "Come on, they're almost here," he added and ran toward the woods. Joe followed.

The bulldozerlike vehicle was plowing full speed up the moutain, its threads throwing up snow in a cloud behind it. Hodges was driving, and the two thugs were clinging to either side.

Frank and Joe ran as fast as they could through the snow. Their enemies spotted them before they reached the cover of the trees, and aimed the Sno-cat right at them.

However, the young sleuths made it just in time and ducked into the pine forest, forcing the Sno-cat to come to an abrupt halt in front of the trees.

The three men jumped off and continued their pursuit on foot.

Frank and Joe ran for a while, then looked back over their shoulders. They saw Ray Hodges, weakened with age, lagging far behind the other two men.

"Let's jump those two," Frank said. "We can ambush them from behind a tree!"

Quickly the Hardys stationed themselves in back of some dense shrubbery and waited for the men to catch up. When their enemies passed, they leaped out from their hiding place and attacked.

"Oooooofff!" one thug cried, catching Joe's flying tackle in the midsection and losing his breath. Joe didn't wait for the man to recover. He quickly delivered a strong left hook to his jaw, then followed with a stunning right jab. The man crumpled to the ground, unconscious.

Frank dealt in similar fashion with the other criminal, and a moment later the second one was knocked out too.

"Now let's get Ray," Frank panted, and started to run back.

Having seen the way Frank and Joe took care of his two cronies, Hodges had doubled back toward the Sno-cat. But instead of remounting the machine, he started up the dark ski slope on foot.

"Where's he going?" Frank wondered aloud, seeing Hodges disappear up the hill.

"I bet he's on the way to the tunnel," Joe said. "Let's get the Sno-cat."

"No, we'd better not. We don't want to alert him that we're coming," Frank cautioned. "Let's walk up. It's not far to the top."

Sneaking up behind the chair lift operator, the Hardys saw him disappear into the cabin at the top station. They tiptoed up to the little building and peered through the window.

"He's not here!" Frank said.

Joe stared. "But . . . we saw him go in!"

Frank nodded. "And I have a hunch where he is. Come on!" He went inside and began to examine the floor of the structure. "Just as I figured," he said and pried open a trapdoor.

"It's the tunnel entrance!" Joe gasped.

A ladder descended down a shaft beneath the floor of the cabin. The boys had no flashlights but decided to climb down the ladder anyway.

After about twenty feet, they reached the bottom and the tunnel opened into a wide, level corridor. A dim light shone at the other end.

"This must be the buried mine shaft," Frank whispered. "Look over there!"

Just visible in the low light were several crude graves lined up near the wall. They were no more than mounds of dirt with simple wooden crosses at their heads. Resting on top of the crosses were miner's helmets.

"The disaster victims!" Joe gulped.

"Let's hope there weren't any recent additions," Frank spoke, worried that one of the graves might contain Richard Chase.

Scarcely daring to breathe, the boys crept past the graves and toward the source of light. There was a bend in the shaft ahead, and the light source seemed to be just around it. As Frank and Joe drew closer, they heard the voices of two men.

"We don't need you anymore!" Ray Hodges said. "Your time is up!"

"Please let me go!" another man pleaded. "I

178

swear I won't tell anything. I swear it!"

On their hands and knees, the Hardys approached the bend in the shaft and peered around it. A single light bulb illuminated the lift operator and another man, who was covered with dirt and grit. His face was filthy and showed a week's stubble of beard. One of his legs was shackled to a chain anchored in the rocky floor. A pick and shovel were leaning against the wall.

"Forget it!" the lift operator spat, taking the heavy miner's pick from the wall. "It's time for you to join my father and the others in their graves!"

With that, Ray hoisted the pick over his head, ready to swing. The shackled man yelped with fear and made a futile effort to protect his face by covering it with his arms.

In the same instant, Frank and Joe dashed at Hodges! He heard the noise and whirled around, trying to aim his blow at the boys. But he was too late. In a flash, he was pinned to the ground.

"Quick, give me your scarf to tie his hands," Frank said to his brother while he sat on the crook.

Not until Hodges was securely tied did the

boys focus their attention on the other man. Then they realized there was something familiar about him.

"You're Richard Chase!" Frank cried, "aren't you?"

The movie actor broke into a grin and extended his hand. "I am. And I sure would like to know who you are. You saved my life!"

20 A Clever Scheme

"That's what we came here for," Frank said, shaking the man's hand. "I'm Frank Hardy, this is my brother Joe, and we've been looking for you for days."

With introductions over, Joe found the key to Richard Chase's leg shackle in Hodges's pants pocket. Once free, the actor assisted the boys in leading Hodges from the mine shaft and out the tunnel. The captive lift operator cursed and kicked as they pushed him along.

Frank went to get the Sno-cat, and then the group headed down the ski slope. They found the two thugs, dazed and shivering, wandering through the snow a short distance from where they had left them. The men gave in easily, and within a few minutes the Hardys had all of the gang locked up in the truck's cargo compartment.

"I thought I'd never get out of there alive," the actor said once he was settled in the cab with the boys.

"Tell us what happened," Joe said, pulling the truck out of the parking lot and heading toward the Adams chalet to see if Chet had gotten safely home from the hotel.

"When I was hired to act in this horror movie," Chase explained, "I did a little research on the outfit. The film's producer, Ian Rider, had some strange people working for him, and he's a bit of a strange one himself."

"His name used to be Larry Hodges," Joe put in. "He's the brother of the man who just tried to kill you."

"I found that out." The actor nodded. "Anyway, I began to check up on him and his company to make sure they were on the level. Then one thing led to another, and pretty soon I was doing a full-scale investigation. I was getting in deep enough that I decided to call your father and hire him to help me."

"And that's when you were abducted," Joe put in.

"Yes. Two men broke into my house and knocked me out with a funny-smelling gas. Next thing I remember is waking up in that mine shaft, where Ray put me to work digging platinum."

When Joe parked in front of the Adams chalet, the Hardys saw lights inside. Chet was there, sitting in the living room and wondering where everyone had gone.

"I suppose Tim and Mr. Adams are still at the police station," Frank said. "Chet, meet Richard Chase."

Chet's eyes popped out. "You found him?"

"In the abandoned mine shaft, which wasn't really abandoned," Frank said and explained to Chet what had happened. Joe, meanwhile, made sandwiches and hot chocolate for all of them.

Richard Chase hungrily ate the food, then agreed to come to the police station with the boys.

"Chet, Richard, and I'll ride in the cab of the truck," Frank said. "Joe, why don't you drive the Ford?"

"Sure will," Joe agreed.

"Maybe Richard would like to wash up first and change into some clean clothes," Chet suggested.

The actor smiled. "That would be great."

The boys lent him pants, a sweater, and a parka, and once he had showered, all four drove to headquarters.

"Who else is involved with Hodges in the film company?" Frank asked the actor on the way.

"Only Bruce, the makeup man, the director, and the truck drivers," Chase replied. "The rest of the crew have no idea what's going on."

"Bruce was driving the Sno-cat when it almost ran over me," Chet explained. "I found that out this evening."

Chase nodded. "Rider was paying the director and the makeup man to help him out. But I don't think even they knew the full extent of the Hodgeses' operation. They just wanted to work, and found themselves having to do more than they bargained for in order to keep their jobs."

The Hardys realized that the producer must have ordered Dutton Foster to cause Tim's accident, in order to escalate the feud. But it was probably Foster's own idea to film Tim's fall when he saw a chance to capture the dramatic incident for the movie.

The small police station was right next to the courthouse. Even though it was well past midnight, the place was humming with activity. A number of cars were outside and lights were on in many of the windows.

After parking the vehicles, the foursome entered the building. There were two jail cells inside, one occupied by Tim and his friends, and the other filled with the townies. Many of the youths' parents were also there, sitting quietly as the sergeant questioned the prisoners.

Frank went up to the officer. "I think we can settle this whole thing!" he announced loudly enough to get everyone's attention. "We found Richard Chase, and if you let me explain, I can prove that the feud was a frame-up right from the very beginning."

In surprise, all eyes turned to the young detective.

"You found Chase?" the sergeant repeated.

"Yes, they did," the actor said. "And the people who captured me are outside in the back of one of the movie trucks."

For a moment, everyone spoke at once, but then a hush fell over the room as Frank told his story. "It all started with a miner named Bill Hodges," he began.

"I remember Bill," one of the men interrupted. "He was the leader of the southsiders who was killed in the mine shaft."

"But what you don't know," Frank said, "is that he stumbled on a rich load of platinum in the mine. He planned to blow up the shaft and dig it out later for himself to get the precious metal. But something went wrong and he was buried along with other workers."

"What!" The people in the room were flabbergasted.

"That's right," Frank said. "The only ones who knew the real story were Hodges's two sons, Larry and Ray. They fanned the flames of the feud to cover up their father's secret and foiled the rescue attempt."

"But what has that got to do with the problem we have today?" the sergeant inquired.

"I'm getting to that," Frank said. "You see, for years Larry and Ray had no way of getting the platinum out of the shaft. The northsiders still owned the mines. When the ski area was built, Ray got a job as a lift operator. Larry moved away, changed his name to Ian Rider, and became a movie producer.

"Ray sat on top of the half-finished rescue tunnel in his lift booth and gradually completed the access to the buried shaft. Larry, meanwhile, was making underworld connections to have the platinum processed and sold."

"This is incredible!" Bob burst out. "You mean, those ghost miners we heard were really the Hodgeses' gang?"

"That's right," Frank said. "They've been working in the shaft for over a year. This winter, they were ready to ship. Larry Hodges picked a movie site nearby and his trucks transported the stuff after it came down the ski lift at night."

"And to cover up their activities," Joe put in, "they used the feud as a diversion. They had to get rid of the man who ran the ski shop, because he was there at night. But they made sure the blame for the fire was put on the boys. That's why they staged all the other incidents like the gas being left on in the general store and the explosion at the mine entrance."

"Mr. Chase had found out a lot about the secret mining operation, so they kidnapped him and then put him in the mine and made him work," Chet spoke up.

"And if the Hardys hadn't rescued me in time, Hodges would have killed me!" the actor said and explained what had happened in the mine shaft.

"And if that doesn't convince you," Frank added with a smile, "we have a load of platinum out in the truck along with the crooks."

After Sergeant Baker inspected the truck's

187

contents and arrested the thugs, Tim and his friends and the townies were set free.

"We'll get after the director and the makeup man right away," the sergeant promised. "And I'll also alert the San Francisco police department to put out a warrant for Ian Rider's arrest."

Frank nodded. He wondered if there would ever be another mystery for them to solve, unaware that soon they would be called upon to work on a case called *Sky Sabotage*.

"Now I want to thank you boys for doing a wonderful job," the sergeant said, interrupting Frank's thoughts.

"So do we," Bret piped up. "I think you stopped the feud once and for all."

"You sure did," Tim agreed. "Because of you, we have a lot of new friends now!" With that, he went around and began shaking the townies' hands. The others followed his example, and soon the solemn gestures exploded into back-slapping, shouting, and laughing, with all the parents looking on happily.

The only one who wasn't entirely happy was Chet Morton, who sat glumly in a corner. "I bet the movie won't be released now," he grumbled. "And I was almost a star!"

Richard Chase put an arm around the chubby

boy. "I'll try to get you another part," he promised.

"Really?" Chet's eyes brightened. "But I think I've had enough of horror movies. Do you think you could make it a detective film?"

Frank laughed. "That's not a bad idea," he said. "Chet has real experience in that field."

SUPERSLEUTHS

by FRANKLIN W. DIXON and CAROLYN KEENE

A feast of reading for all mystery fans!

At last, the Hardy Boys and Nancy Drew have joined forces to become the world's most brilliant detective team!

Together, the daredevil sleuths investigate seven spine-chilling mysteries: a deadly roller-coaster that hurtles to disaster, a sinister bell that tolls in a city of skeletons, a haunted opera house with a sinister curse — and many more terrifying situations.

Nancy Drew and the Hardy Boys — *dynamite!*

Armada

Kay Tracey Mysteries

by Frances K. Judd

Look out for Armada's fantastic new detective series!

Kay Tracey has an uncanny talent for solving clues and unravelling baffling mysteries. Don't miss her first two thrilling adventures.

1 The Double Disguise
2 In the Sunken Garden

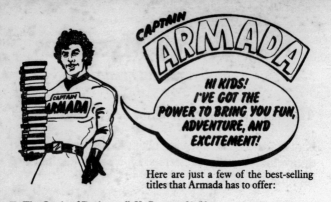

CAPTAIN ARMADA

HI KIDS! I'VE GOT THE POWER TO BRING YOU FUN, ADVENTURE, AND EXCITEMENT!

Here are just a few of the best-selling titles that Armada has to offer:

- ☐ The Castle of Darkness *J.H. Brennan* £1.50
- ☐ Anyone Can Draw *Introduced by Tony Hart* £1.25
- ☐ The Funniest Funbook *Edited by Mary Danby* £1.25
- ☐ What Katy Did *Susan M. Coolidge* 95p
- ☐ A Fresh Wind in the Willows *Dixon Scott* £1.25
- ☐ Ten Ponies & Jackie *Judith M. Berrisford* £1.25
- ☐ The Mystery of the Scar-Faced Beggar
  Three Investigators Series £1.25
- ☐ The Emperor's Pony *Ann Sheldon* £1.25
- ☐ The Wizard of Oz *L. Frank Baum* 95p
- ☐ Little Men *Louisa M. Alcott* £1.25
- ☐ Shadow the Sheepdog *Enid Blyton* £1.25

Armadas are available in bookshops and newsagents, but can also be ordered by post.

HOW TO ORDER
ARMADA BOOKS, Cash Sales Dept., GPO Box 29, Douglas, Isle of Man. British Isles. Please send purchase price plus 15p per book (maximum postal charge £3·00). Customers outside the UK also send purchase price plus 15p per book. Cheque, postal or money order — no currency.

NAME (Block letters) _____

ADDRESS _____

_____

_____